WILL KEEN

THE LAST CHANCE KID

Complete and Unabridged

LINFORD
Leicester

First published in Great Britain in 2003 by
Robert Hale Limited
London

First Linford Edition
published 2005
by arrangement with
Robert Hale Limited
London

British Library CIP Data

Keen, Will
    The Last Chance Kid.—Large print ed.—
    Linford western library
    1. Western stories
    2. Large type books
    I. Title
    823.9'14 [F]

ISBN 1–84395–765–5

Published by
F. A. Thorpe (Publishing)
Anstey, Leicestershire

Set by Words & Graphics Ltd.
Anstey, Leicestershire
Printed and bound in Great Britain by
T. J. International Ltd., Padstow, Cornwall

This book is printed on acid-free paper

THE LAST CHANCE KID

When Lane Condry, The Last Chance Kid, paid a rare visit to the family home in Arizona's San Pedro Hills, he found his younger brother, Nate, acting suspiciously, and the property being threatened by unscrupulous mine owner Jack Kenyon. Then his father was wounded in a dawn attack by Kenyon and the owlhoot Colquhoun clan. But even worse, Lane found himself falsely accused of murder and sent to prison. What hope did he now have of establishing his innocence and meting out justice to the owlhoots and murderers?

Books by Will Keen
in the Linford Western Library:

HIGH PLAINS SHOWDOWN
STAND-OFF AT BLUE STACK
THE DIAMOND K SHOWDOWN

Prologue

In the cool hour before dawn, the mist came down over the high ground and chilled him to the bone. Grey and moist, it writhed around the jagged rocks to cut through the thin shirt and worn denim pants given to him by the prison guard Nate had bribed, and drop a thin veil over the distant, barely distinguishable lamps of the Yuma State Penitentiary. It dimmed those faint yellow lights and, like wads of cotton stuffed in his ears, it deadened or distorted all sounds. The far off, plaintive cry of a coyote that had marked the long hours of his wait was suddenly fainter than the ragged whispering of his pulse and, to his straining ears, every muffled sound became the snort of an approaching horse, every click of a shifting rock the faint rattle of its hooves.

Teeth chattering, Lane Condry, The Last Chance Kid, wriggled stiffly into the notch he had chosen for his vantage point and, from under the pulled-down brim of the stained and battered Stetson the guard had thrown in as an afterthought, squinted down and to his left. Half a mile away, a couple of hundred feet below the rocks, the dry wash was now no more than a vague dark patch like a stain spreading away from the high ground, quickly fading beneath the spreading blanket to become part of a flat, grey landscape. Around and beyond it, as he stared, shapes moved eerily. But it was the mist, that was all. Shifting, drifting, eddying in currents of air that, over the desert's ridges and pockets, ran cold, then warm. He squeezed his eyes shut, opened them and saw nothing but patches of the featureless Arizona terrain, the vague shapes of giant saguaros stretching their arms to the unseen stars.

Nothing stirred.

'Wait there,' Nate had said. 'Keep your head down, don't move away no matter what. I'll be there before dawn with a good horse, food, a six-gun. I cain't do no more, but I figure it's enough to see you across the border. It's a chance, maybe the last you'll ever get, kid . . . '

Enough? Sure it was. And any chance was better than no chance when a man's facing twenty-five years in the pen for a crime he didn't commit. But because this was likely to be the last chance for a man who'd faced more than a few of those in his time — and here the kid allowed himself a thin smile — he'd taken one look at the dry wash when he came hobbling out of the arid wilderness that lay between him and Yuma, and walked away.

A man who's spent even a short month locked in a jail cell has already developed a morbid fear of enclosed spaces.

But this time he walked only far

enough to find a lofty vantage point where he could hole up and watch, because he'd already walked three miles. Maybe more. Jesus, when had he ever walked that far! Walked, and run. Heading east, across the northern edge of the Yuma Desert. And after all that effort still too close to the pen to consider himself safe, or beyond the reach of the hunters.

He rolled on to his back on the slabbed rock, automatically reached into his shirt pocket for tobacco then realized who he was and what he was wearing and laughed bitterly out loud — and at once clamped his teeth on the sound and went still, ears straining in the sudden, aching silence.

Escaped convict. Wearing another man's shirt and pants. His whole future in his brother's hands. And behind him, the sky already lightening as the unseen sun floated up behind the Gila Mountains to the east and began painting the high thin clouds with washes of pink and gold.

'Come on!' he whispered. 'Goddam-mit, Nate, move yourse — '

There!

He rolled over, dragged himself into the notch with his clothes catching on the rough ground and peered between the rocks and over the edge. Everything below was cold and empty, blanketed with that thin mist that made a mockery of a man's eyes, still untouched by the high reflected light of the rising sun.

But now . . . now there was a sound.

And the kid's stomach knotted and his mind went cold and empty as he listened, for what he was hearing was not the comforting jingle of a bridle, the creak of saddle leather, but the swelling beat of hooves as a number of horses approached — not fast, for he was on foot and there was nowhere for him to go even if he could have outpaced them — but with a relentless pounding that had the finality of nails being driven into a rough pine coffin.

His mind raced, screaming silently

for reassurance. Hell, Nate was coming for him, bringing a horse, that was the arrangement. So why panic? Wasn't that what he was hearing? His brother was drawing near, not hurrying, pushing easily through the thinning mist, riding one horse and leading another. Yet even as his mind grasped at that thin straw his hand was sliding instinctively to his hip in the manner of someone who has grown up wearing a six-gun, and when it found there nothing but the smooth worn cloth of another man's pants he felt the cold sweat break out on his forehead, and in his breathing there was the sudden tightness of fear.

Now he could see them. The mist had thinned considerably. The sun's light was beginning to flood the land. He counted three, four . . . then two more. Six riders. They rode towards the dry wash in extended line. As he watched, pulse hammering, the flank riders pushed ahead so that the line became a rough curve that would envelop the entrance to the shallow arroyo. In the centre, a man held back. He reached down, straightened, and a rifle's long barrel flashed cold and deadly in his hands. A big man, straight and tall.

And as the Last Chance Kid watched the Yuma posse close in on the dry wash he had turned his back on, from that tall figure sitting straight in the saddle he heard, in the silence of that fateful dawn, the musical ching of Mexican spurs.

Part One

The Arrest

1

Eight weeks earlier, Lane Condry had ridden home from Tombstone to the San Pedro Hills with a head that was muzzy from the effects of too much strong whiskey, but a mind clear enough to appreciate that his pa was in deep trouble — and anything affecting old Ben Condry was certain to cause his close-knit family a whole lot of grief.

Lane had been back in Arizona Territory just two weeks, after a year drifting across southern Texas, and had spent the evening in the Eagle Brewery on Fifth Street. He had spoken to acquaintances and friends, but mostly he had listened keenly to the buzz of conversation, glass in hand, back to the bar, eyes hooded, a lean man doing some hard drinking and keeping himself to himself.

Appearances were deceptive. His place at the bar had been deliberately chosen. He had positioned himself within earshot of one particular table and, as cigarette smoke became a pall hanging under the gilt oil lamps, and the free flow of strong drink turned talk into a raucous clamour that pained the ears, it was on that table that his attention was concentrated.

Three men, expensive whiskey, a pack of cards. Men with crisp white shirts stretched over burly frames and sprinkled with the ash of fat cigars. Black string ties loosened beneath jowls glistening with sweat. Crystal glasses in hands accustomed to counting dollar bills, cards fanned in fingers on which gold rings glittered, but at which dark eyes that were shrewd and calculating glanced only occasionally. For these men were gamblers who played for stakes far above those associated with their game of five card draw, deuces wild, and the ruthlessness that was hidden beneath the exterior of businessmen playing convivial poker meant that the talk to which Lane Condry listened was laced with evil intent.

Back in the 1850s, Lane's pa, Ben Condry, had moved West and begun raising cattle along the San Pedro River. It had been a struggle, but he'd made a living, and in time his pretty young wife had brought two fine sons into a world full of promise. But that promise had gone up in smoke with the arrival of violent, lawless men who had the same idea as Ben Condry but made the work easier and more profitable by bringing in rustled beef from Mexico. Wisely, Ben had moved his family away from the river up into the San Pedro Hills and, on land less favourable for the raising of cattle, had taken to breaking horses for sale to a US Government struggling to feed the Apaches on the San Carlos Reservation. Again, hard work ensured that the enterprise kept his family from starving, but that one forced move was more than enough for a man who had already travelled a thousand miles from his birthplace; he vowed to his wife and growing sons that, for him, the next move would be when they carried him off in a box.

All this had been long before Ed Shieffelin was scoffed at by scouts from Fort Huachuca in the Apache country for prospecting in that part of south-eastern Arizona — all he'd find, they told him, was his own tombstone — and had then gone on to find silver-bearing ore in the foothills of the Dragoon Mountains and stake the claim that was to become the town of Tombstone. And if Ben Condry had ever been disturbed — as he surely had — by the conviction that the one-room timber shack that had spread in all directions to accommodate his growing family would, one day, stand in the way of ruthless businessmen hungry for a slice of the silver bonanza, he had always managed to hide his uneasiness.

For Lane Condry, on that evening of drinking and listening in the Eagle

Brewery Saloon, the terrible weight that must have rested on his father's shoulders for so many years was becoming clearer by the minute.

The card-playing, whiskey-drinking businessmen who sat in their chairs within spitting distance of Lane Condry, were a motley crew of fat cats and killers sharpening their claws before pouncing on the next mouse. The mouse was Ben Condry. The motive was silver. The outcome — to these men — was never in doubt.

'If our mutual friend doesn't come up with something, we could always try buying out Condry.'

This was Jack Kenyon, a mine-owner who had dealings with owlhoot elements, and with Sheriff John Behan. His list of confidants and associates suggested the lawless were balanced by the law-abiding but, in Tombstone, it meant no such thing. John Behan was a peace officer with a flexible frame of mind. He had a tolerant attitude towards Arizona rustlers and, in the months before the gunfight at the OK Corral and its aftermath drove Wyatt Earp and Doc Holliday to New Mexico, he would happily deputize the owlhoot Clanton brothers as highly efficient enforcers.

'Why bother?' The speaker was Lee Kenyon, Jack's hot headed son. Squinting through the smoke from his cigar he was built like his father, but the heavy frame was less muscular and was padded with the soft flesh that comes from easy living. 'He'll haggle. All that does is waste time, and in the end you know damn well what it'll boil down to — right, Abe?'

'Use of force?' Abe Colquhoun was a wolf dressed in sheep's clothing, a rustler who mixed with Tombstone's elite while making his living selling stolen cattle through Bauer's Market. His big fists bore the scars of countless bar-room brawls. The pistol at his hip had a butt worn smooth by frequent use. An owlhoot who had drifted down to Arizona Territory from Kansas when the cattle drives coming up from Texas no longer offered rich pickings, he and his sons, Seth and Quent, had jumped up in status after the murderous gunfight at the OK Corral and taken over the mantle once worn by the infamous Clantons and McLowrys. The Colquhouns were cattle rustlers with the demeanour of respectable citizens; hired killers at home in arroyos or dark alleys; and because they would switch sides if the balance of power shifted, they were unpredictable, and doubly dangerous.

'Right,' Lee Kenyon said. 'The only way is to go in hard, and go in now,' and he frowned irritably as his father shook his head.

'We wait to see if our friend comes through. If not, we talk to Ben Condry. Only then do we — '

'Pa, you're wasting time.'

Jack Kenyon grinned. 'Playing safe. One step at a time. It made me rich, and one day it'll all be yours.'

'Then let's take Ben Condry now,

and double my inheritance.'

'No!' Jack Kenyon snapped the word, and his son sat back in his chair, face flushed, eyes ugly.

Sickened, scarcely able to believe what he was seeing and hearing, aware, too, that Jack Kenyon had for several minutes known that Ben Condry's son was at the bar and listening, Lane tossed back his drink and headed for the doors. They slapped behind him as he stepped out and took a deep breath of the cool of the night, disgusted at the sour taste of whiskey and the raw bite of cigar smoke in his lungs. But the discomfort in his body was as nothing to the slow fury burning in his mind at what he had overheard and, as he stepped away from the Eagle Brewery, unhitched his horse and swung into the saddle, he was already composing the bitter message he would pass on to his pa when he reached home — and wondering what the hell good it would do any of them if they were forced to defend themselves from the raw violence of Abe Colquhoun and his two wild sons.

* * *

The stars were sprinkling a clear moonless sky with their brilliance when he rode up the steep, twisting trail and passed through the natural fault in the hillside and on into the broad hollow where Ben Condry had built a second home for his family. At once, the half-broken horses in the corrals sensed his presence. Vague, shadowy shapes moved. One of them gently whickered, and he caught the smell of them mingled with the dry taste of drifting, kicked-up dust.

Familiar lamplight welcomed him as he rode past those sturdy corrals and on towards the house, spilling from yellow squares of curtained warmth that were windows to the life of comfort and security he had enjoyed since he was a kid in short pants. Safe in the hollow, he found it impossible to

19

believe that everything Ben Condry had built up was now in danger — yet there was no mistaking the message in Jack Kenyon's words. Lane clamped his jaw, biting back the anger, then took a tight breath and let it go explosively. It helped — but not a lot. There was a job to be done, bad news to be delivered. Determined to get it over and done with, he off-saddled, dumped his rig over a pole in the barn, let his mount loose in the smaller corral at the other side of the yard and slammed the pole into place.

Then he paused, braced himself mentally and physically and went into the house.

His first impression was of his mother's face. All three of the big room's occupants turned to look at him as he entered — his brother Nate, long, gangling, lean face dominated by his dark, dragoon moustache, stretched out in a chair near one of the oil lamps leafing through a copy of the *Daily Epitaph*; Ben in his customary position alongside the stove with his battered Stetson on, wide red galluses holding up his work pants and his grey eyes squinting against the acrid smoke from the pipe that was permanently clamped in his strong white teeth. But it was his mother's perceptive blue eyes that took one look at him and immediately registered alarm. Lane saw at once that she had detected something in his manner, his bearing, and suspected something was wrong. Her face visibly paled. The dishes she was about to carry from the table to the small kitchen rattled as a tremor passed through her slight body.

'Oh my God!' she said softly, and hastily put the dishes back down as if they had suddenly become red hot.

Lane flipped his hat on to a hook, and forced a smile.

'A cup of that coffee'd go down well, Ma.'

'Before you fall over?' Ben growled.

'I'm not drunk.'

Nate chuckled. 'A man comes back

to home territory after a spell away, only natural he enjoys himself.'

Nan Condry shook her head. 'He's been drinking, but he's clear headed. He's been in the Eagle for a good reason — I know, because he told me before he rode out. Now there's something troubling him . . . right, Son?'

'Ma, I really would like that coffee before we begin to talk the night away.'

'Must be mighty serious,' Ben said around the stem of his pipe, 'if it'll take that long.' But his voice was too casual, and suddenly there was the chill of carefully guarded apprehension in his eyes.

'If he's been in the Eagle,' Nate said, 'he's been close to a heap of trouble.'

'The Colquhouns?' Lane nodded. 'Abe was there, for sure. Talking to the two Kenyons.'

He had moved away from the door. Nan was at the stove, filling a cup with scalding black coffee. Ben had taken his pipe out of his mouth and was absently

22

rubbing the side of the bowl with his thumb.

'Go on,' Ben said.

'From what I overheard, we're in a heap of trouble that has more to do with Jack Kenyon than Abe Colquhoun,' Lane said and, as he took the coffee from his ma, he felt the tremor in her hand and noted — without comment — the sharp, sidelong glance she cast in Ben's direction.

'And why would that be?' This was Nan again, sitting now, both hands flat on the table. 'What have we done that has any connection at all with that . . . that black-hearted businessman and his dim-witted son?'

'What we've done,' Lane said, 'is get on the wrong side of the wrong people by building our home in the wrong place.'

'And to that,' Ben said, 'you get my usual answer: I moved my family once because of the Clantons and McLowrys. The next time I move — '

'Yeah,' Lane said, his irritation

softened by affection. 'It'll be in a pine box. Well, let me tell you, Pa, if Jack Kenyon wants that silver bad enough, that's the way you'll go.'

'And does he?' said Nan.

'There were three men around the table. They knew I was there, and it made no difference. Why should it? Me listening to every word spoken has saved them the effort of sending a messenger.' He met his mother's troubled gaze, pressed on relentlessly. 'A mutual friend was mentioned. The suggestion was this feller might come up with something. Pa, you got any ideas on who that might be?'

Ben grunted. 'A friend of that crowd ain't worth knowing,' and Nate laughed softly.

'If that fails, one of them suggested they pay us to leave. That was Jack Kenyon. His son didn't take him seriously, and also didn't see the point in wasting time and money. Abe Colquhoun was keeping his head down as always, but — without committing himself — seemed to go along with Lee Kenyon's opinion that the only way to move us is at the point of a gun — or several of 'em.'

Lane pursed his lips, and stared bitterly into the coffee cup. When he looked up it was to complete silence. But the expression on his father's face was unchanged.

'Let them come,' he said, and then a thin, humourless smile flickered as he lifted the briar pipe and, with clear intent, levelled it like a six-gun at the darkness beyond the window.

'You figure we can hold them off?'

'You said I built this house in the wrong place. I know what I did was right. Sure, it may be sittin' astride a vein of pure silver. But it's set in a hollow, the only easy way in's through that notch and, yeah, I reckon me and Nate can hold off an army of Colquhouns — leastwise until Sheriff John Behan gets wind of what's afoot.'

'Lane's here,' Nan said, her eyes on her younger son. 'He's home for a while now, and he'll do more to help us than that excuse for a lawman.' Suddenly, her voice was derisive.

'Behan's straightened himself out now the Earps have gone,' Ben said.

'But if this mysterious friend can't work whatever magic he's up to,' Lane said, 'and you stand firm, hold out against Kenyon's cash offer — '

'Ain't enough of the stuff been minted,' Ben said scornfully.

'Then, after that, the violence could come at any time.'

Ben frowned. 'Let's get this straight. From what you overheard you figure Jack Kenyon's after a seam of silver running smack dab under this house. There's a suggestion of a feller we ain't set eyes on who's trying to work something for him, if that fails Kenyon's going to make a cash offer, and when I turn him down flat he'll use them damn Colquhouns to run us off the land.'

'Right.'

'So we go to Behan now.' Nan's face

was stubborn as she recommenced clearing the dinner-table. 'Forewarned is forearmed. Maybe he'll go talk to Kenyon. If he's threatening us — '

'He's not,' Lane said. 'Not yet.' He watched his ma leave the room balancing plates on a crooked arm, turned to his pa and went on, 'If I tell Sheriff Behan what I overheard he'll likely refuse to confront Kenyon. If he does go see him, the man will call me a liar — and then we've forewarned the wrong man.'

'Don't matter.' Ben stood, stretched, yawned. 'Kenyon can call on the Colquhouns for help, and, well, he's a hard nut with a big shotgun — but I've cracked tougher.'

'Happier, Ma?'

Back in the room, wiping her hands, Nan looked at her son and shook her head. 'No, Nate. Lane came home with bad news, and all you and your pa have done is *talk* your way out of trouble. You're both good at that — but this time I can't see it working.'

And as Lane Condry drained the last of the coffee, he knew that his mother's words were the only ones that made any sense. Trouble was brewing and, one way or another, the Condry family would get sucked into the violence and bloodshed.

2

Lane spent a restless night, tossing and turning as the moon slanted cold light through the gap in his curtains and the soft sounds of uneasy horses in the corral added weight to the crawling fears that refused to go away.

With that peculiar, inbred sixth sense that could always be trusted, Ben Condry's wild horses knew something was wrong and, over and over as he lay on his back and stared into the chill half light, Lane listened to them and cursed his haste in walking out of the Eagle.

Sure, Ben Condry was right. They would hold on to what was rightfully theirs, and if, in the event of an attack, Sheriff John Behan was slow in coming to their aid — and he was bound to be, considering the distance between Tombstone and the San Pedros — then it was down to Ben and his two sons.

The fact that they had right and the law on their side was, to Lane's way of thinking, irrelevant — and his thinking was coloured by what he had seen and heard. He had leant against the bar in the smoke and the din of the Eagle Brewery and listened to Jack Kenyon and, as the mine-owner spoke to his two cronies, Lane had looked covertly into his eyes and been shocked by what he saw. Without doubt, Kenyon was the man to fear. He had been talking merely to air his thoughts, and the other opinions voiced around the table — though listened to with commendable politeness — were so much wasted breath. The man's mind was made up, and if any single comment had affected him, it had been Abe Colquhoun's. 'Use of force?', Abe had said, and though the remark had been posed as a mild question, for Jack Kenyon it had been the match that lit a short fuse.

At that point, Kenyon had been unable to hide his feelings. The flare of excitement in the man's eyes had been no figment of Lane's imagination. Colquhoun's words had convinced the mine-owner that the time to act was now, the way to act was with the use of brute force — and what better time to strike than in the hour before dawn?

Lane's thoughts, those, but likely to be on target for he knew what made these men tick and his thinking was indelibly coloured by tales from the past. Kenyon and Lane's pa were of an age, and it was Lane's pa, the old soldier, who had planted that idea of a swift dawn strike in his head, many times relating to his wide-eyed sons how Civil War battles had been lost and won by the use of such tactics, and how George Armstrong Custer had defeated Black Kettle of the Cheyenne by riding in with his 7th Cavalry across the snows of a crisp and misted Washita dawn.

So those powerful images and the gnawing conviction that he was right inevitably went with Lane Condry into an uneasy sleep that carried him from moonlit darkness to the cold clear light that precedes that vulnerable hour. And, just as inevitably, he was snapped out of that sleep by the whip-crack sound of a pistol shot and was out of his bed and grabbing for his gunbelt as the reverberations echoed around the hollow and faded away into the encircling San Pedro Hills.

* * *

The shot sent splinters flying from the gallery of Ben Condry's sprawling house, and when Lane Condry exploded through the front door he was met by a second bullet that kissed the side of his face with its hot breath before slamming into the log walls.

He ducked back, saw the brooding Quent Colquhoun holding a smoking pistol and his brother Seth laughing fit to bust as their horses circled. Abe Colquhoun was off to one side, long grey hair ragged beneath his greasy Stetson, a rifle resting across his thighs. Jack Kenyon was across the yard close to the corral, a black-suited, powerful figure atop a big sorrel and outlined against the hills. A Greener shotgun jutted from his saddle boot.

'That's enough!'

It was Kenyon who had spoken and, as the mine-owner nudged his horse forward, Lane saw Nate come around the corner of the house, tall and lean in pants and undershirt with a pistol in his fist and his face split by a broad grin.

Then Ben Condry was striding across the living room. A heavy gunbelt was buckled about his thick waist. His face was an expressionless mask. He pushed past Lane, stepped out on to the gallery.

'Those Arizony rustlers the best you can come up with, Kenyon?' he said with a contemptuous sweep of his arm.

'They'll serve a purpose.'

'Which is?'

'You're in my way.'

'I've been here twenty years — and now I'm in your way?'

'Times change. Successful men move with them.'

'Or get greedy.'

Kenyon shrugged.

'Is that it? I'm in your way?' Ben laughed. 'Hell, coming from you, that won't even spoil my breakfast.'

'If you're still around this time tomorrow,' said Quent Colquhoun, 'the only thing you'll be tastin' is hot lead,' and Seth's wild laughter rippled across the yard.

'That a fact?' Ben's voice was flat. He gave Quent scarcely a glance. Staring hard at Kenyon he said, 'Is that what this is about? You want me to up stakes, move my family out of their home so's you can dig yourself another mine?'

'Silver's my business,' Kenyon said. 'Yours is selling half-broken horses to the army. Whatever arguments you come up with to hang on here, a calculating man looking at priorities would give them short shrift.'

'Lordy, just listen to the man,' Lane said. 'He rides out at dawn, spouts words clever enough to confuse a lawyer when all he's doin' is actin' like one of them goddamn rustlin' Colquhouns.'

'It appears,' Jack Kenyon said, 'that words of any kind are wasted here. But let's spell it out anyway, in the hope that you'll see sense. Condry, you know what I want. You've got until dawn tomorrow to get out, kit and caboodle. If you're still here at first light you'll be moved by force, your house will be demolished and my gangs will move in to commence digging.'

'Maybe,' Ben Condry said through his teeth, 'but you won't be here to see it.'

His hand was moving as he spoke, dropping to slap leather and grab for the butt of his heavy Dragoon Colt. But he was slow. The six-gun was dragged from a holster stiff from lack of use, by a hand gnarled from years of hard work.

Across the yard, Quent Colquhoun moved with lazy speed. He'd let his

35

gunhand relax, allowing his packed fist to rest on his thigh. Now, seemingly without haste, he lifted it and snapped a shot in Ben's direction.

The bullet slammed into the horse trader's right shoulder. He took a stumbling backward step. The Dragoon clattered to the boards. Caught in the narrow doorway, blocked by his pa's bulk, Lane could do nothing. He had time and space enough to see Seth Colquhoun draw his Colt, Jack Kenyon reach down and smoothly pull the big Greener shotgun from its oiled boot.

Then Ben Condry's sagging bulk was heavy in his arms and, as Lane turned with him, lowered the groaning man to the floor and felt the warm wetness of blood on his bare hands, Nan Condry was running across the room and stooping alongside her stricken husband with soft, wordless murmurs of distress.

Tight-lipped, holding the hot anger in check, Lane stepped outside. He pulled the door to, keeping his hand clear of his holster. At the corner of the house, Nate was standing with his hands level with his shoulders, palms forward. He looked calm, relaxed. The grin had gone, replaced by a faint smile. He looked at Lane. As he did so, his right hand moved up and down in a calming motion. Meant for Lane? Or for somebody else? If so, who? Lane wondered about that. Then the oily click of hammers being cocked pulled his attention back to Jack Kenyon. In the mine-owner's dark eyes there was a blatant challenge. No, Lane thought, not a challenge. The man's hungry. Blood's been drawn, he's fired up with the smell of it . . .

'You want to finish it now, Condry, make my job easy?'

'Faced down by three outlaws, a man holding a cocked Greener?'

'Your choice.'

'Right now we've got no choice.'

'I'm glad you understand that. The only thing you've got wrong is the timing. For you Condrys, here in the San Pedros there's never going to be a choice. Leave now, while the going's good, or leave belly down. Every damn one of you.'

With those final bleak words, Jack Kenyon lifted the reins high and spun the big sorrel. Then, shot-gun held out to one side, he kicked his horse into a gallop and rode away across the yard. He was followed by the three Colquhouns, and mine-owner and rustlers sent the nervous wild horses racing away from the rails with heads tossing as they hammered past the corral and dragged a swirling trail of dust towards the notch in the hills.

3

They used the battered old buckboard
to take Ben Condry the long haul into
Tombstone, the bandaged horse trader
sitting upright but white-faced on the
seat alongside Nan as she pushed the
rattling wagon along the rutted trails at
a pace that allowed her husband some
relief from his agony, but ensured a fast
trip.

Lane and Nate rode behind, not
doing much talking but keeping their
eyes skinned the whole time in case the
Colquhouns decided an ambush would
solve Jack Kenyon's problems and save
them a second trip out into the hills
and a risky shootout.

When they hit an area of foothills
split in several directions by arroyos and
dry run-offs, Lane spoke briefly to send
Nate ahead, then slowed his own pace
until he was a couple of hundred yards

behind the wagon. He figured that if they were about to be dry-gulched, then this was the most likely spot and it was prudent to get spaced out. An hour later, when the wagon bounced and trundled on to flatter ground and the danger was past, they kept to that formation and Lane rode relaxed in the saddle and alone with his thoughts.

Mostly he thought about his pa. It was late October but the sun was already high, the heat blistering, and the dust kicked up by Nate's horse was a thin dry cloud drifting back towards the buckboard through air that shimmered. The wounded man would be weak and dizzy, the sweat and the dust combining to cause him considerable discomfort. But with a hot surge of pride that brought a lump to his throat, Lane knew that a short spell of acute suffering was unlikely to faze a hard-working man who had gone for his six-gun when three of the armed men he faced had weapons in their hands.

Lane's feelings towards his pa were a mixture of that warm and justifiable pride at his courage and indomitable spirit, disbelief at his recklessness, and frustration at the impossible circumstances that had forced the old-timer to risk his life. For, if not in the wan light of that day's cool dawn, then surely the showdown would come at the next. Hadn't Jack Kenyon told them that, warned them that if they were still occupying the hollow when twenty-four hours had passed, they would be forcibly moved on? And hadn't Ben Condry told his family — time and time again — that the only way he would move from their home in the San Pedro Hills would be in a wooden box?

Lane was again swamped by feelings of immense pride when he looked beyond the buckboard to where his older brother, Nate, rode ahead of the thin dust cloud with his head constantly turning as he watched for trouble. From childhood he had been courageous without being hot headed, and possessed of a rare intelligence. That precious attribute had stayed his hand when his pa had gone for his gun and, while the Colquhouns might have looked on it as a display of cowardice, Lane knew that the decision had been calculated, and right. One man had taken a bullet in the shoulder; a shootout with all guns blazing would have resulted in a bloodbath.

At twenty-eight, Nate Condry was a credit to his father, a fine and loyal son, and he had acted in the best interests of the whole family. And yet . . . there was that strange moment in the lull after the pistol had cracked and Ben Condry had fallen, the signal from a smiling Nate that was clear in its message — easy now, cool down, that's far enough — and, disturbingly, could have been telling Lane not to react, or telling the Colquhouns and maybe Kenyon himself that enough was enough.

And, to that second thought with all its sinister implications, Lane Condry deliberately blanked his mind.

It was close to noon when they clattered into Tombstone. They came together on the town's outskirts, swung the buckboard around to Dr Gillingham's and eased Ben down from the seat and into the office. Nan stayed with him. As the door closed, Lane climbed back on to the buckboard, Nate rode behind leading Lane's horse, and in that fashion they made their way through town to the corral owned by Sheriff Behan.

Somebody else had the same idea.

Abe and Quent Colquhoun must have dropped in at their spread on the river after the gunplay in the hills, picked up a buckboard and come in the easy way. Their team was already unhitched and loose in the corral, the wagon up against the barn. Abe was talking to the hostler. Quent had wandered away and had a boot heel hooked on the corral's lower rail as he leaned back and smoked a cigarette.

As Lane pulled the buckboard to a halt, Nate rode alongside, slipped quickly from the saddle and said, 'Do we talk to them?'

'Waste of time.'

'Hell, without Kenyon standing by we've got a chance to get our point across, warn them if they don't back off — '

'It was Quent did the shooting, he's already gone that one step too far — '

'But if we can talk Abe round, Quent will follow his pa.'

'Better if we let things lie.'

'How come?'

Lane watched Quent push away from the corral, flick his cigarette into the dust, then join Abe and stand talking. He thought they looked uneasy. That, or fired up, riding high on a rush of bravado.

'Think about it. They're as likely to shoot as talk, and if they take us now, it's over.'

Nate laughed. 'I think Abe's forgot all about this morning, he's in town to get himself well and truly sodden.'

'And Quent?'

But Nate was no longer listening. Quent Colquhoun had looked over, and now he flicked a hand in greeting.

'Mornin', Quent,' Nate called. 'Seth around?'

'Later. We've got cash due from Bauer's Market.'

'You tellin' me you get paid for those cattle you steal?'

Colquhoun grinned. 'You watch your tongue, boy,' he said easily.

He turned away with a ching, ching of big Mexican spurs, and a moment later he and Abe left the corral. Lane dealt with the hostler, making sure he knew that the buckboard would be needed if Ben Condry was well enough to head home, and leaving his and Nate's personal mounts to be off-saddled and let loose in the corral. He spent a few minutes telling the old man what had transpired out in the San Pedros and, after accepting his commiserations, left the tiny office.

Nate was already walking away.

'What the hell was going on back

there!' Lane said, as he caught up.

'Being civil. Nothing wrong with that.'

'After what they did?'

'You said let things lie.'

Lane grunted. 'Well, maybe I don't like the idea of you consorting with men who shot down your pa — '

'Jesus!' Nate said in disbelief. 'You say one thing and mean something else, is that it?'

'No, it's not, and saying howdy ain't sitting in a feller's back pocket, I know that.' Lane rested his hand on Nate's shoulder as they walked on. 'I'm touchy, boy. You can't blame me for that.'

Nate tossed him a quick grin, but it didn't quite reach his eyes and, as Lane let his hand fall to his side, he knew the vague unease he felt wasn't about to go away. There had been a casual familiarity between Quent and Nate and, for the first time, Lane found himself wondering what his brother got up to on his visits to Tombstone. And suddenly, unbidden, he again recalled Jack Kenyon's brief mention of a mutual friend . . .

Experiencing a feeling of intense guilt, he tried unsuccessfully to dismiss his suspicions as unfounded and disloyal, and led the way up Allen Street where Nate called in at the Pioneer Boot and Shoe Store. Lane knew he would spend time there, the young feller being somewhat fussy over the quality of the boots he purchased and, telling him they would get together later, he walked on.

The town was hot and dusty, wagons trundling through the ruts, and townsfolk, miners and cowboys going about their business among the various retail establishments. A wagon team was being unhitched at the OK Corral, the teamster cursing as he struggled with the lathered horses. Dust rose in clouds. Coughing, Lane spat drily, pushed on by and made for Fifth Street. The saloons were already open for business. He glanced across at the

Eagle, decided that he'd had enough of the place after the previous night's poisonous talk, and crossed the street to the Oriental.

It was almost empty, dim and relatively cool after the heat and glare of the street, the still air thick with the smell of stale drink and cigarette smoke. Brass and glassware gleamed and sparkled in the gloom. A man in a white shirt and black pants was sitting at a table, bootlace tie dangling as he leaned over a game of solitaire. His moustache had a flamboyant sweep. His eyes were almost luminous as he looked up at Lane, then went on dealing the cards.

At the bar, Lane ordered a glass of beer, then reviewed the possibilities. Nate was busy most of the time, a tall, lean man and just about the best horse breaker Lane had come across. His trips to town were regular, but infrequent. So if he was involved with the Colquhouns, it would likely be through playing poker with the brothers — no more than that. No consorting with outlaws. No involvement in what had happened that morning. And if anyone knew anything about gambling in Tombstone, it would be Ace Jardine.

Beer in hand, Lane crossed to the table where the man was studying the layout.

'Mind if I join you?'

Jardine looked up. 'No, so long as you don't jump in and tell me this card goes here, that one there.' He lifted a hand to the barman. 'This social, or business?'

Lane smiled. 'Bit of both, I guess.'

The barman arrived, placed a jolt glass on the table, drifted away. Jardine lifted it, tossed back the raw spirits, squeezed his eyes shut for a moment then nodded at Lane. 'Fire away.'

'You know my pa?'

'We've met.'

'He's over at Doc Gillingham's, being patched up. Quent Colquhoun's work. Him and Seth, and their pa. They rode out to the San Pedros at dawn, called in with a warning.'

'Not enough brains between the three of them,' Jardine said.

'No, they were provided by Jack Kenyon.'

'Ah.' Jardine nodded understanding. 'He's expanding his interests, and Ben Condry's spread's in his way.' He shrugged. 'Why come to me? Shouldn't you be talking to Johnny Behan?'

'Knowing Behan, I think that might be a waste of time.'

'So?'

'So if Behan's out, we're forced to go it alone.'

'Might be tough.'

'I'm thinking of the indirect approach.'

'And talking in riddles.' Jardine placed an eight of hearts on a nine of spades, turned the next card. 'But I can see your point about Behan. He could pull Quent Colquhoun in, but Kenyon would deny responsibility — deny even bein' there.'

Lane finished off his beer and nodded slowly. When he walked into the Oriental his mind had been on Nate. He'd seen Ace Jardine and broached this subject on the off-chance, with maybe something working at the back of his mind, the glimmer of an idea. And still, he thought ruefully, he hadn't put his question to the dapper gambler.

His chair scraped as he pushed it back and, as if on the spur of the moment, he paused and said, 'If a man wanted a good, honest game of poker, would he come here, or go across the road?'

There was a wariness to Jardine's smile. 'You've ridden a hell of a way for an answer you could get back home.'

'What — Nate?'

Jardine shrugged. 'Ask him.'

'Ask me what?'

Both men snapped their heads around. Unnoticed, Nate Condry had slipped in from the dust and dazzle of the street and was a tall figure standing in the shadows to one side of the swing doors. Instantly, Lane's senses were heightened, his mind sharpened as it raced hither and yon seeking ways to justify or exploit the situation, and sought to recall spoken words. Memory came to his aid, and with it some relief: it was Ace Jardine who, without committing himself, had nevertheless pointed the finger at Nate.

'Mister Jardine,' Lane said, 'is of the opinion you know where I can find a good game of poker.'

Nate laughed. 'You talkin' that way's about as natural as a leopard fixin' himself new spots. You decided to do some of that consorting yourself, Lane?'

'If it gets me close to the Colquhouns, to Jack Kenyon — yes, I think I have.'

Glass clinked as Nate collected a drink and turned to stand with his back to the bar.

'Is that wise?'

'How's Pa?'

Nate laughed. 'You read me like a book.' He took a drink, nodded. 'Sure, I went back. He's fine, all fixed up. Ma's figurin' on takin' him back home herself.' He waited for Lane's reaction, saw none and said, 'What about this card-playin'? You figure getting close to those fellers will give you some kind of influence. Or are you hoping to catch the big mine-owner cheating, find an excuse to gun him down?'

Lane left the question unanswered as he walked to the bar with his empty glass. His mind was still chasing shadows, but now it had direction and purpose. The idea that had been but a glimmer had suddenly burst into flame, the casual question about his brother's nocturnal activities bringing closer a way of talking to Tombstone's lawless elements without arousing suspicion, and of getting close enough to Jack Kenyon to look into his soul. What good it would do he did not know, but in the time they had left he had to do something. It was already past midday. Ben Condry had a plugged shoulder, a warning hanging over his head that was a threat to his whole family. If Kenyon returned at dawn as promised, they had less than eighteen hours.

'Getting too close to the Colquhouns,' Jardine said from the table, 'could be a mighty perilous game.'

There was sudden amusement in Nate's eyes. 'Then I suggest you be there to watch the action.'

'Wouldn't miss it,' Jardine said. 'And in case you still don't know — and your kid brother decides to keep quiet — I know Jack Kenyon'll be in the Oriental with a sealed deck of cards sometime after midnight.'

'Nate?'

'Oh, I'll be there.'

'Then it's best if Ma takes Pa home in the wagon.' Lane toyed with his empty glass, then pushed it away decisively. 'We already discussed this last night,' he told Nate, 'and it's already started. Kenyon's got the Colquhouns backing him, and he's got his pick of a bunch of tough mine workers. If one of us doesn't stop him before dawn tomorrow, he'll ride in with his crew and every damn one of us Condrys could be six feet under.'

4

Sprawled on the hard cot in the boarding-house room he'd booked into, Lane Condry spent that long, sweltering afternoon in Cochise County, Arizona Territory, feeling like a man trapped in a Dutch oven. He sweated, he dozed, only to awake an hour later with his shirt wet with sweat and the dust of Allen Street drifting in through the open window — and all the time, asleep or awake, he was suffering the torments of indecision and doubt.

There was doubt, because he knew he was not qualified to judge his elder brother. Nate had been a home boy all his life, and had worked alongside his pa from the winter day when — as Ben told it — he had cracked the yard's thin ice with his first steps and sat down in the cold water. Lane, two years younger and somewhat in the shadow of the

56

stalwart man to whom Ben looked likely to pass on the mantle of family patriarch, had been a drifter who had spent more time away from the San Pedro River — and, later, the hollow in the hills — than he had spent at either of those homes. Restlessness, and the conviction that there was more to life than getting his brains scrambled atop a succession of sunfishing broncs, had time and again driven him away from the home spread. He had always returned for a spell of six months or so to clean the poison of a succession of honky-tonk saloons, Mexican cantinas and flea-infested lodgings out of his system with some good, honest toil, but on those occasions his pa had worked alongside him with one jaundiced eye on his wayward son and had eventually, in exasperation, given him a moniker that had stuck.

'I'll give it one more go,' Lane would drawl, when the itch got too stong. 'Drift down to Texas, give it one last try. Cross the border into Mexico, hunt for

Montezuma's gold.'

And so he became the Last Chance Kid, and because one last chance always led to another he matured the hard way in the rough territory he frequented and pushed on into his twenties, lean and sharp-eyed and greased lightning with a six-gun. The name went with him. Somehow, what had been born out of his own determination to give himself one more chance to find a life to which he was suited became the code by which he lived. He found those words spilling unbidden from his lips when he was faced by hard-eyed gunmen anxious to pit their skill against his: 'One last chance to back off, feller . . . I'm giving you just the one chance to turn around and ride away from here . . . This is your last chance . . . ' until the name coined half in jest by his family became one he was feared by in those border towns, where it acquired a new and deadly meaning.

He had become a gunslinger by accident, with a reputation based on hearsay, but if his exploits were shamelessly embellished around countless smoking camp-fires, it was certainly true that he was a man who had honed his six-gun skills to perfection, and who was more familiar with the horses he had ridden back and forth across a dozen ill-defined borders than with the rawboned brother he loved dearly, but did not understand.

But if that was true he thought, standing stripped to the waist and glistening with sweat at the boarding house window, if he knew horses but not his own flesh and blood — why the suspicion? Was it *strong* enough to be called suspicion, or was it no more than instinct honed by those sojurns in one-roomed adobe cantinas where smoking oil lamps coated the beams with black grease and a gringo was wise to sit with his back to the wall? Did he know that something was wrong — but not know why he knew? And if that was the extent of it, was he right to do what he was about to do? Was he right to think of sitting across the table from his brother in a card game with some of Tombstone's crazy owlhoots just so he could watch, wait, and listen?

And so the indecision.

Which, like most products of a man's muddled thinking when, in any circumstance, he sits and whiles away lonely hours, was of his own making and misguided to boot. The truth was he was about to sit in on a poker game in the Oriental saloon because he wanted to get close to Jack Kenyon, the man about to run the Condrys off their land. No other reason — or none he was prepared to admit to. If Nate was there, and trouble exploded, he would back his brother to the hilt. And when the Last Chance Kid turned away from the window to check the loads and the oiled action of the six-gun that lay on the bed, to slide the gleaming pistol in and out of the supple leather holster, his hands were slick with sweat, but steady, for he knew that he could wish for no more able partner.

5

The cards snapped. A low voice said 'Call'. A second man raised, and there was a soft curse from the first man and a slap as his cards were flung down. A glass clinked as another man lifted it to his mouth to drink, was betrayed by the tremor in his hand and said huskily, 'I'm out.'

Money jingled as it was raked in by the winner. A chair creaked as a player turned, gestured to Ned Boyle, the Oriental's barman, who reached behind him for a bottle. At the table a match flared.

Two o'clock in the morning. Quent Colquhoun, his brother Seth, Ace Jardine. Abe Colquhoun at a nearby table nursing an almost empty bottle of whiskey and switching his bleary gaze between the smoking oil-lamp above the card table and the circle of players.

Sheriff John Behan a white-shirted figure outside the circle of light — for, at Quent Colquhoun's request, all lights had been extinguished save for that solitary lamp. Nate Condry, eyes bright, his lips under the flamboyant dragoon moustache wearing the suggestion of a smile.

Jack Kenyon.

The Last Chance Kid.

Tension was like the shimmer of thin smoke in the room. Ace Jardine was relaxed, a professional gambler who took the rough with the smooth, rode the highs and lows that came with the game of poker. Jack Kenyon was winning. Others around the table were ice cool, or glistening with sweat, depending on their temperament, or the quantity of hard liquor they'd poured down their throats.

John Behan was odd man out, the sheriff of Cochise County who had wandered in for a late jolt of Ned Boyle's finest and stayed to watch the game's ebb and flow. Though outside the circle of light cast by the single oil lamp he was still too close for Abe Colquhoun's comfort, and the snap of cards and the murmured bids had been a counterpoint to the sporadic insults and threats tossed back and forth in the shadows by Colquhoun and Behan.

What Lane Condry had not seen in all the time he had been sitting at the table was any suggestion that Nate was on friendly terms with the Colquhouns. What he *had* seen — or at least come to suspect as the hands were played — was that Jack Kenyon was cheating.

And with that nagging suspicion that over the hours gradually strengthened to become a conviction, Lane knew he had been given a weapon he could use against the big mine-owner.

They were playing five-card stud. Players were dealt two cards in the initial deal, one face down, one face up, then three more exposed cards in successive deals leading to a final showdown. Tough to cheat unless you were dealing, though there were more opportunities as the night dragged on and weariness and alcohol began to dull the senses. A non-dealer who set out to cheat would have several opportunities to change his unexposed hole card: during each deal he could contrive to cover the hole card as he received the next exposed card, and substitute a palmed card. Changing a single exposed card, as it was dealt, was almost impossible. Almost, Lane thought, as Nate shuffled the pack, then executed a noisy riffle. Almost, because with a fast dealer, distraction as the card was dealt and lightning fast reflexes, a hand could dart out to cover and replace the new card — before it was identified by others — with one held in the palm.

The next deal gave Lane the opportunity to sit back and observe.

Quent Colquhoun was next to Lane on his right, Kenyon across the table. Nate was next to Colquhoun. He dealt smoothly and fast, giving each player one card face down, the other exposed.

The cards whispered slickly from the pack held in his left hand, each one a blur as it skimmed low across the table.

Quent's exposed card was a nine. Lane got an exposed two and had a concealed three, and knew he was finished. On his left, Jardine had an exposed eight, next to him was Seth Colquhoun with an exposed ace. Across the table, Jack Kenyon had a six face up.

Seth was high with the ace, and bet, but reluctantly, suggesting he had nothing in the hole. Kenyon, Nate and Quent Colquhoun called, Lane threw in his hand with a grimace and Seth called.

The second deal gave Quent Colquhoun a jack, Jardine got a seven, Seth a two alongside his ace and Kenyon a second six. Nate dealt himself a king. The concealed cards were telling no tales, but Jack Kenyon now had an exposed pair.

So, as high man, it was Kenyon's bet. Nate immediately raised, and with grunts of disgust Quent, Jardine and Seth threw in their hands. Kenyon called, and Lane figured that the mine-owner had more than his two exposed sixes. Had more — or was about to switch his hole card.

Nate's next deal gave Kenyon a three, himself a nine. No improvement on the table. Kenyon checked, Nate bet, and Lane guessed his brother had a king in the hole. But would that pair be enough to beat Kenyon, with a small pair exposed?

Kenyon at once suggested it wouldn't: he raised, and Nate, figuring he was trapped but reluctant to fold, called.

His last deal did nothing. An ace to Kenyon, an eight to himself. That left Kenyon with two sixes, a three and an eight exposed, Nate with seven, king, nine and eight. Kenyon bet. Nate called, and the mine-owner flipped over his hole card to reveal a third six. Without a word, Nate tossed in his hand. Kenyon raked in the small pot, and Jardine took a breath and shook his head.

Lane had seen nothing irregular. Kenyon's big hands had been on the table. At times, the one hand had partially covered his face-down hole card. But had he switched? As Nate shuffled, Lane caught the mine-owner watching him. For an instant their eyes locked and, as they did so, Kenyon almost imperceptibly shook his head.

Meaning what? The mine-owner was no fool, and he would know that there was a connection between what had happened at dawn and Lane's appearance at the poker table. So what was he saying with that faint shake of the head? That Lane was wrong, he was not cheating? Or was that negative shake a reminder of what would happen at the next dawn — just a few short hours away? A reminder that the Condrys were finished?

Abe Colquhoun cut through Lane's thoughts, kicking his table aside with a swinging boot as he rose to his feet and stumbled to the bar with the empty bottle swinging from his fist. John Behan was also up on his feet. Across the darkened room his eyes bored into Colquhoun's back as Ned Boyle produced a fresh bottle. Then he lowered himself into his seat, but in such a way that his jacket was swept back and his right hand free to reach his pistol.

'You with us?'

That was Nate, deck of cards poised, watching him.

'Go ahead and deal,' Lane said, and flicked a glance at Kenyon. The big man grinned and shrugged, then reached for his glass as the cards began to fly, ostentatiously sitting well back in his chair.

Lane's hand was a bust. He got a three and concealed two to Quent Colquhoun's exposed king, and knew he was out. Seth was dealt a face up two, Nate dealt himself an ace face up, Jardine a five, Kenyon a jack.

With the ace up it was Nate's turn to bet. He did, Quent stayed, Lane and

Jardine folded. Seth and Kenyon both called.

The next deal left Seth Colquhoun looking bad with a two and three exposed. Kenyon wasn't much better with a seven to go with his jack, Nate got a six alongside his ace, Quent a ten with his king. So there was no change for the better on the table, and Lane felt a pulse beat in his throat as he looked at the concealed cards in front of the four remaining players. What had Kenyon got hidden? Would it improve on his jack and seven? Or would he need some sleight of hand?

It was impossible to tell from the betting. Nate placed a bet, Quent Colquhoun called, as did Seth. Kenyon raised — but was that bluff, a safe bet on what he had concealed, or a bet because he intended to improve his hand by cheating?

The raise drove Seth out. Nate and Quent Colquhoun called, watching Kenyon.

The next deal left Kenyon and Nate

without improvement, giving them a nine and a two respectively. But as the cards came to rest, Quent had two tens in front of him — the winning exposed hand.

Again, Lane looked at Jack Kenyon. Quent had a pair, but he could have another ten in the hole. Kenyon had nothing on the table — but what about his concealed card? The best possible was a pair of jacks, which would beat Quent. But Nate had an ace on the table. If he had another in the hole, there was nothing Kenyon could do.

Yet when Quent Colquhoun bet on his two tens, Kenyon again raised.

Nate folded. He'd had no ace in the hole.

On Nate's next deal, Quent got a final four alongside his pair of tens: no improvement. But when an ace flicked out to settle in front of Kenyon, Nate gave an explosive snort of disgust, and slapped the deck down hard.

It was a natural reaction, because the ace would have helped him. It was of no use to Kenyon.

At that point, with Jardine looking mildly amused, Seth now away from the table and at the bar alongside his pa, and Quent Colquhoun's head turned to watch both of them, Lane caught a sudden flicker of movement as Jack Kenyon reached out to straighten the face-up ace.

Then both the mine-owner's hands were withdrawn.

Quent checked. Kenyon bet. Quent called.

Kenyon flicked over his concealed jack to make a pair, and raked in the money.

'You cheated,' Lane said softly.

A challenge couched in the softest of terms will alert those men attuned to the nuances of hard talk. At the bar, Abe and Seth Colquhoun went still, then turned slowly. Nate's face hardened. Alongside Lane, Quent Colquhoun slowly eased back his chair.

'Say again,' said Jack Kenyon.

'You cheated,' Lane said, and he

kicked back his chair and rose to his feet. 'You had a jack palmed, and switched your hole card.'

'When?'

'As you took that final ace.'

'Why would I do that?'

'To win the pot.'

'Colquhoun had two tens exposed. He could have had a third in the hole, and I'd have wasted effort giving myself a second jack, at one hell of a risk.'

'I wondered about that. Why would a man like you risk his reputation for a few dollars? And then I realized that a man with your power doesn't like to lose, won't accept losing — ever.'

'Back off, Condry,' Jardine said. 'Apologize, then go home while you're still able.'

'Kenyon used a palmed card — '

'You're wrong.' The dapper gambler's tone was flat, final.

'If the man's innocent, it's too late for apologies.' At the bar, Abe Colquhoun was standing spread-legged and unsteady alongside Seth, the full bottle of whiskey clutched against his chest. 'Condry accused a good man of cheatin'. Only one way that can be settled.'

The mine-owner was sitting back, at ease and unflustered. He raised an eyebrow at Lane. 'What about that, Condry? What's this in aid of, what do you want from me?'

'Lane,' Nate said urgently, 'you watch your back,' and Lane realized Quent Colquhoun had pushed his chair all the way back from the table and was on his feet.

At the same time, with Kenyon's questions hanging in the air and Lane honestly unable to answer, Abe Colquhoun had shrugged off Seth's restraining hand and moved away from the bar. He was closer to the table. The hand holding the whiskey bottle had dropped to his side.

The questions hung unanswered. A silence had fallen over the room, raising the tension. The initiative was slipping away from Lane. Kenyon had backing, his demeanour suggested innocence. Lane was isolated, with nowhere to go, no way out. The silence dragged on. He felt cold sweat in the small of his back, the sudden dryness in his mouth that told him he'd dug himself into a hole.

He met the mine-owner's derisive gaze, saw the half smile on the man's lips and began to lift his hands in what he knew would be a futile gesture of conciliation — and Abe Colquhoun drew his hand high and back and flung the full whiskey bottle.

It spun in a glittering arc, smashed into the oil lamp over the poker table and dowsed the light. The room went black. Glass and coal oil rained down on the table. Someone yelled and a chair scraped and went over with a bang. There was a thump, somewhere overhead.

'Light, Ned!'

Kenyon, yelling to the barman in a voice tight with sudden panic. There was an answer that Lane didn't catch, then a curse and behind the bar glass shattered. A match scraped, failed to light. Then someone on Lane's right — Quent Colquhoun? — bumped him heavily. A hard hand grasped his forearm, clamped tight, held him steady. At the same time he felt a hand fumble at the holster tied to his right thigh. He tried to twist away, but the hand stayed clamped on his arm. There was an oily click, and Lane felt the hairs on his neck prickle.

Then a six-gun blasted.

In the blackness, the muzzle flash was dazzling, its after-image a lingering red flare. The crack of the shot died flatly. A man gasped, as if in sudden agony. The clamping hand fell away from Lane's arm. He stepped back, stabbed a hand for his holster, expecting to find it empty. His six-gun was there. He closed his fingers around the warm butt, drew, turned towards Quent Colquhoun — and someone at last found a usable lucifer.

The match flared. A second swiftly followed. Seth Colquhoun had lit the first, and turned to hold it high as Ned Boyle fired up the second and applied it to a lamp's wick. In the feeble light that was as bright as day after the blackness, a stark tableau was cruelly exposed.

Lane was standing back from the poker table, his six-gun in his hand with a wisp of smoke curling from the muzzle. Quent Colquhoun had stepped away, and was staring at him. Neither Nate nor Ace Jardine had moved from their chairs. And Jack Kenyon would never move again. The big mine-owner was slumped back in his straight chair. On the front of his white shirt, bright red blood glistened wetly. His eyes stared sightlessly but accusingly across the table at Lane Condry.

And as the first match died and the oil lamp in Ned Boyle's big fist cast its brightening light over that scene of violent death, from his table outside the circle of light, cocked six-gun in hand, Sheriff John Behan said, 'Nobody move.'

6

'It's been fired,' John Behan said and, as he spun the six-gun's cylinder and ejected the single empty shell, he met Lane Condry's eyes.

'Not by me.'

'It was in your hand, and a man lies dead.'

Lane looked across to where Seth Colquhoun stood at the bar, the lamp on the counter bringing out glittering highlights in the shotgun's barrel.

'If my pistol's been looked at,' Lane said to Behan, 'all weapons should be checked.'

Behan nodded. 'That will be done. But Abe Colquhoun's unarmed, I know Jardine's not carrying, so I'd say you're running out of alternatives.'

'Dammit!' Lane said, 'I didn't shoot Kenyon. When the lights went out I was jostled from the side. Another man used the darkness to kill Kenyon with my Colt.'

'The only man close enough,' Abe Colquhoun said, 'was my boy Quent.'

'I was too busy ducking away from the action,' Quent Colquhoun said. He stepped forward, drew his six-gun and banged it on the table. Glass from the shattered oil-lamp crunched, and Nate protested softly as a shard flicked against his cheek.

'I didn't touch Condry's pistol,' Quent said. 'There's mine. Check it now, and let me get to bed.'

Still seated opposite Nate, Ace Jardine took the pistol, sniffed the barrel, spun the chamber. He looked at Behan, and shook his head.

With a snort of disgust, Quent picked up the pistol and wiped coal oil from the barrel on to his pants, pouched it, and made for the door. It slapped behind him as he went out into the night. In the silence they could all hear the ching, ching, ching of his Mexican spurs as he stepped down from the plankwalk and crossed the street.

Swiftly, efficiently, John Behan checked the remaining weapons. None had been fired, and now Seth followed his pa out of the saloon. Nate shook his head, rested his hand on Lane's shoulder and muttered, 'Everything'll be fine,' then walked out of the Oriental.

'Ned,' John Behan said, 'get on over to Ritters, tell them to send a hearse for Kenyon.'

'You need Doc Gillingham?'

Behan shook his head. 'No. I reckon we can all see he's dead. But you'd best run over to the jail, get the city marshal over here so the arrest is official.'

The bartender left with his message for the marshal and the undertakers. Behan pouched his six-gun, went behind the bar and returned with a fresh bottle of whiskey in one hand, three jolt glasses on the fingers of the other. He sat down, upended the glasses and splashed whiskey into them, jerked his head at Lane.

His mind racing blindly down trails that led nowhere, Lane sat down. He took a glass, downed the strong spirit, felt the prick of tears that were part despair, part the reaction to the raw liquor. The light from the oil lamp on the bar cast a circle of light that fell short of the poker table with its litter of broken glass, slicks of coal oil and the discarded playing cards. As Ace Jardine leaned forward to toy restlessly with the cards, the light gleamed eerily on his pale face.

'So, Condry,' Behan said, 'you found your own way of dealing with Jack Kenyon.'

'No. It was made to look that way.'

'Why the hell would anyone do that?' said Jardine.

'Kenyon was after the silver buried under Condry land,' Lane said. 'The Colquhouns were his muscle. But I can't see why they turned on him — unless someone else wants Kenyon's mining company, and the silver under my pa's land.'

'Your brother had good reason to want Kenyon dead,' Behan said.

'We both did — but that doesn't make me a killer.'

Behan shook his head. 'I'm not talking about Kenyon's push for Condry land.'

'What, then?'

Behan looked at Jardine. 'You sat in on most games, Ace. How much was it?'

Jardine shrugged. 'Over a spell of six months, I'd say close to ten thousand.'

'What?' Lane looked at the watching faces, the flat, impersonal expressions that gave nothing away, the blank eyes that concealed a wisdom picked up through bitter experience in lawless frontier towns, a knowledge that when the chips were down and men's backs were against the wall even the most outrageous became not just possible, but almost inevitable. 'What!' he said again in astonished disbelief. 'Are you suggesting Nate framed me, his own brother, to wipe out his gambling debts?'

'Maybe not that,' Behan said, 'but he is your brother so it gives you another damn good reason for pulling the trigger.'

As the words that pointed to the hopelessness of Lane Condry's situation hung in the smoky air of the Oriental, Jardine eased himself up from the table and, with a wave of the hand to John Behan, made for the door. It swung open as he reached it, and Ned Boyle came in followed by the bulky figure of James Grey, the city marshal. After that everything went too fast for Lane. Grey listened to an account of the events, formerly arrested Lane, took him to one side as a bleary-eyed employee of Ritter and Ream's undertakers arrived to take care of the body, charged him with the murder of Jack Kenyon and marched him down the centre of the street to the jail.

Within thirty minutes of Kenyon's death, Lane was locked in a strap-steel cell, sitting on the hard cot with a tin plate of grub at his feet and his head in his hands. It was approaching three o'clock, the square of sky visible through the high barred window still dark but with a suggestion of the lightness that would herald the approaching dawn. He didn't know if Nan had taken the wounded Ben Condry home to the hollow, didn't know where Nate had gone; didn't know if Jack Kenyon had issued orders to his tough mine workers that would see them — despite his unexpected absence — already riding hard towards the San Pedros to drive the Condrys from their home and burn down their property.

Certainly Lee Kenyon would be keen to take over that part of his father's operations, even if less inclined — or equipped — to take over the running of the mining empire.

Lane didn't know who had set him up. He couldn't understand why it had been done. His attempts to get close to Jack Kenyon had ended in disaster, far from helping his family he had left them with a man short when he was most needed, and although he had learned something about Nate, that knowledge was now worthless. All Lane Condry knew for certain on that cold, early morning was black despair. He was accused of murder, he was a few short hours away from being taken before Judge Wells Spicer for what looked like an open and shut case and immediate conviction — and he could see no way out.

7

The coldness of the desert night outside the jail was like a grim harbinger of death so that, in his lonely torment, Lane Condry imagined the icy breath of the grim reaper himself seeping in through the high barred window. With no blanket to warm him, he lay rigid and shivering on the cornhusk mattress. With no pleasant thoughts to occupy his mind he constantly relived the shattering of glass, the dazzling muzzle-flash splitting the blackness, the dark wet blood on Jack Kenyon's shirt as, at the bar, Ned Boyle applied flame to the lantern's wick; the circle of accusing eyes looking at the still smoking six-gun clenched in his fist.

Part of his torment lay in the knowledge that his unfounded suspicions had put his family in jeopardy, left them without his help when they most needed it. If he had not become fixated with thoughts of Nate's treachery — or that he was, for some reason, consorting with unsavoury characters — he would not have sat in on that fateful poker game. If he had not gone to the Oriental, he would have left Tombstone early and been home for supper with Nan and Ben. And if he had done that — and slept in his own bed — he would have been there when Jack Kenyon rode into the San Pedro Hills with his tough mine workers as dawn broke.

With a start, Lane twisted his head to look at the window.

And saw — with a sudden quickening of his heartbeat — that it was now a pale square perceptibly lighter than the darkness of the cell.

He sat up on the crackling mattress, swung his legs over the edge of the cot. His booted feet hit the hard dirt floor. He stood up, crossed to the window, reached up with both hands to grasp the cold bars and peer at the lightening sky; turned away with a gasp of frustration.

With Kenyon dead, who would lead the mine workers into the San Pedros? Was there anyone to take the dead man's place, or would the move to expand his mines fizzle out as others fought for control of his interests? Lee Kenyon was his father's natural successor. But were there others in Cochise County prepared, and able, to fight the younger man — and win?

Lane began to pace: five steps one way, turn, five steps back.

Maybe, in his stupidity, he had inadvertently become his family's saviour. The conversation he had overheard in the Eagle suggested that Jack Kenyon was in absolute control of his companies, Lee Kenyon violent and hot-headed but no businessman, others not mentioned — shadowy figures on the outer fringes — willing to take their cut for favours granted, but too busy with their own interests to become actively involved in the mining of silver.

The most likely result of Jack Kenyon's sudden demise was a swift takeover by other mine-owners with the ready cash to dazzle the dilettantish Lee Kenyon. They would seize their chance, the fast return from taking over Kenyon's holdings — and doubling their profits — preferable to the long wait required before seeing any return from the ore beneath Ben Condry's land in the San Pedros.

The question was, Lane Condry thought, had Behan or anyone in the know — Abe Colquhoun, perhaps? — moved fast to drag some muzzy-headed businessman out of bed and give him the news of Kenyon's death, and the opportunities it opened up? Would any business deal be in time to halt the raid to drive the Condrys out that was due to take place at dawn?

And — and this was a sudden appalling thought that sickened him, stopped him in his tracks and left him a shallow breathing, shrinking shadow in the cold centre of the strap-steel cell

— would he be alive to see the answer to any of those questions after the city marshal, James Grey, had marched him in front of Judge Spicer and related how Lane Condry had accused a prominent businessman of cheating and, seconds later, been caught with a smoking six-gun in his fist and that man lying dead before him?

8

As it transpired, it was some time after that fateful dawn that Lane Condry was taken before any judge, and when he did make his appearance it was at the court of Justice of the Peace A. O. Wallace.

He was given breakfast by a deputy at the jail, was allowed a wash in cold water but no shave, then listened to the clang of the door being locked and settled down to cool his heels in the cell. Strangely, the onset of daylight had brought some relief. Though his situation was in no way improved by being able to see the interior of his prison — stone walls, a filthy mattress, strap-steel bars through which a bare interior room with table and oil-lamp were visible — a calmness had settled over him and he was able to put aside all despairing thoughts. Indeed, it was as if thoughts of any kind had flown like startled birds. He dozed, or simply sat on the cot, arms wrapped around drawn-up knees, and stared into space through half-closed eyes.

It was at those times when, somewhere between sleeping and waking with his mind treading water and most receptive to whatever thoughts might be lurking beneath the surface, Lane Condry truly believed that the course of a man's life was preordained, and that he would never be convicted of a crime he did not commit.

At about 11.30 he heard a ruckus somewhere out in the street. He was at the bars looking out but able to see nothing but a stretch of clear blue sky when the deputy arrived at the cell with a jingling bunch of keys, and escorted him to the front office. Marshal James Grey was waiting.

'What's going on?'

Grey shrugged. 'Abe Colquhoun treading on a few toes, Quent trying to sort him out.'

'That man shot Jack Kenyon, should be in here, not me.'

Grey's face was impassive. 'Tell that to Wallace.'

'Wallace?' Lane felt a sudden flicker of dread. 'Where's Judge Spicer?'

'Out of town.'

'But Wallace has no authority.'

'You can tell him that, too.'

With the deputy along as armed escort, Grey marched Lane into the street and they made their way to the Courtroom. Inside the dusty building, a sick-looking Seth Colquhoun was mopping blood from his head with a handkerchief, another deputy standing close by. Grey sat Lane down inside the railings, leaving the deputy by the door, hand close to his six-gun.

They waited for several minutes. The two deputies got together and, from what he managed to overhear, Lane worked out that Colquhoun was being charged with carrying a weapon inside the town limits. He managed a rueful grin that was caught by James Grey, whose jaw tightened. It was a law that was enforced arbitrarily. Done according to the book, it would have seen Lane in the Oriental unarmed, Jack Kenyon would be alive, and Lane would now be riding towards the San Pedros.

Some five minutes later, an inner door opened and Justice of the Peace Wallace came through followed by a clerk. Grey looked at Lane, shook his head.

'Colquhoun first, then you — but I guarantee you won't get off with a fine.'

Wallace was dark and balding. He sat down at one end of a long desk, the clerk at the other, listened to the deputy then looked with a thin smile at Seth Colquhoun's bleeding head and fined him on the spot for carrying firearms within the city limits. As Colquhoun turned away with a snarl of anger, Quent Colquhoun came in, spurs jingling, took the situation in at a glance, and went to Seth.

'What the hell happened?'

'Never mind. Let's get out of here, go see Doc Gillingham.'

'Cash first,' said Wallace.

Glowering, Quent Colquhoun paid his brother's fine to the clerk and went out with Seth. The second deputy waved a hand, and followed.

Wallace turned to James Grey. 'This Lane Condry?'

Grey nodded, and Wallace switched his gaze to Lane.

'Sheriff John Behan's already apprised me of the situation, of what occurred in the Oriental Saloon. Since then I've spoken to witnesses — '

'My brother, Nate Condry?'

'No, but Ace Jardine was at the scene — '

'Did he tell you the lamp was out, nobody saw what happened?'

Wallace frowned, and looked at Grey. 'That right?'

'So I've been told. According to John Behan, Condry shot Kenyon when Abe Colquhoun smashed the lamp.'

'Somebody shot Kenyon,' Lane said. 'Not me.'

'I've also spoken to Quent Colquhoun,' Wallace said. 'He was involved in the game, saw everything.'

Lane's laugh was bitter. 'He was close enough. But I've told you, there was nothing to see. Like Grey said, the place was in darkness when Abe Colquhoun smashed the lamp.'

'But when Ned Boyle lit a replacement lamp, you were standing with a smoking weapon in your hand, and Jack Kenyon was dead.' Wallace let his chair swivel, away, then back. 'You deny that?'

Lane shook his head.

'Aloud, please.'

'No, I don't deny it.'

Wallace looked at the clerk. 'You getting all this?'

The clerk, bent over an impressive looking folder, pen in hand, said, 'Yes, sir.'

To Lane, Wallace said, 'If you don't deny that, then the rest follows logically.

You went to Ace Jardine and told him of some dispute between your family and Jack Kenyon. Mr Jardine has also told me that, before last night, you had never taken part in a poker game in Tombstone. Yet you sat in on this one, accused Jack Kenyon of cheating — and subsequent examination of the dead man, and the deck of cards, proved without doubt that he was playing a clean game — and when Abe Colquhoun smashed the lamp you chose that moment of confusion to murder one of Tombstone's most prominent businessmen.'

'Somebody else,' Lane said desperately, 'used my gun to kill him.'

'Plucked it from your holster, fired, and replaced it?'

'Yes.'

'And you allowed that to happen?'

'I was taken by surprise.'

Wallace leaned back, gnawing at his lip. He looked at James Grey and said, 'Does this feller's story make any kind of sense?'

'No, sir,' Grey said. 'He's come up with a story, and he's sticking to it — but why would anyone do that? *Who* would do that? — use Condry's six-gun to kill Jack Kenyon?'

Wallace nodded slowly, steadily, and there was a hollow feeling in Lane's stomach as he saw a look of grim resolution harden the man's eyes.

'The Last Chance Kid,' Wallace said, 'isn't that what you call yourself? You have a reputation. I admire your father, Ben Condry. He's a fine, hard-working man, but you are a footloose drifter who helps him only when it suits you.'

'I did not kill Jack Kenyon.'

'The evidence — '

'I was framed.'

' — says you did. By the authority vested in me by Magistrate Court Judge Wells Spicer, in his absence I have the power to convict. I do that now, and for the cold-blooded murder of Jack Kenyon I sentence you to twenty-five years in Yuma — '

'You can't do that. I'm entitled to a fair trial!'

'This hearing is fair. I am a Justice of the Peace, Mr Grey is an officially sworn-in lawman, my clerk is recording the proceedings. Swearing in a jury would waste good men's time, bring the same result. You have the right to appeal when you get to Yuma. It'll get you nowhere.'

'Jesus Christ!' Lane said. 'You're sending an innocent man to — '

'Take him away, Mr Grey.'

The heat hit Lane like a hammer as they stepped out into the street. Feeling sick to his stomach, he stumbled after the deputy and James Grey, not knowing where they were taking him, not caring. So much for optimism, for an innocent man's belief that his voice would be listened to, his word accepted. The worst had happened: in the space of ten short minutes he had been convicted of a crime he did not commit and sentenced to spend most of his adult life in the state penitentiary.

And it was now almost midday. He still did not know what had happened at dawn out in the San Pedro Hills.

The three men were walking in line, Grey leading, Lane just behind him with the deputy taking up the rear. They were heading back towards the jail. Around them the bustle of a working day in Tombstone brought the rumble of wagons, the cries of teamsters, the whinnying of horses and clogging clouds of dun-coloured dust. Stunned by the hand fate had dealt him, Lane walked with his head down. Then James Grey stopped abruptly. Lane blundered into him and was rewarded with a soft curse, a word of reprimand from the deputy. But both were halfhearted.

When Lane looked up he saw they had reached Fremont Street near Third, facing down towards Bauer's Union Market. The Colquhouns — Abe, Seth and Quent — were standing on the corner of Fourth Street and Fremont and, as Lane watched, they moved towards the market and began an angry confrontation with the proprietor. He recalled the words exchanged between Nate and Quent yesterday — Lord, that long ago! — and remembered that Quent had said the Colquhouns had cash coming for the sale of cattle. It seemed now that the market's owner disputed that claim — and the argument was getting more heated.

'Goddamn!' James Grey said softly. 'That looks like trouble.'

With a quick word to the deputy, he crossed the street and ran towards the bunch of men outside Bauer's. The deputy drew his pistol, cocked it, rammed the muzzle into Lane's back and said, 'Move yourself.'

And suddenly, Lane Condry's heart was thumping.

Just the one man guarding him — and they were heading towards the busiest part of town.

A second, painful prod from the pistol forced him to begin walking. He kept his pace slow, guessing that for some way the deputy would be glancing over his shoulder, craning his neck to watch James Grey and the Colquhouns. And while they walked, Lane's mind was racing. If he was going to make a break, it had to be now, or never. With the jail drawing closer with every step, he was unlikely to get a second chance. But the deputy was a tough-looking character with a cocked pistol in his hand and the sense to have dropped back a couple of paces so that he was well out of Lane's reach. And Lane wasn't sure if he could rely on the Tombstone people to stand by and do nothing while a prisoner escaped.

Where was the second deputy, the man who had been escorting Seth Colquhoun? He had followed Colquhoun when his fine had been paid, and had probably headed back towards the jail — another reason for Lane to make his break now!

But if he got away, where would he go? Home? Pulling an angry posse towards the San Pedros? No! Ben and

Nan had trouble enough, and if there was ever a time to move on, it was now.

Now, now, now! The word kept hammering at Lane's brain, emphasized by each soft thump of his boots in the dust as he walked steadily towards the Tombstone jail and twenty-five years incarceration in the state penitentiary.

Where, he wondered bitterly, was Nate?

And then all thoughts were wiped from his mind as they crossed a narrow side street alongside a general store and a rider came hammering out, tried to pull up and the rearing horse's flashing hooves came between Lane and the startled deputy. Caught by a hoof, the lawman staggered back, cursing. His arm flew high to ward off another blow. The pistol cracked, the bullet winging skywards. Close by, a woman screamed.

Lane broke, and ran.

Behind him, horse, rider and deputy were still tangled, the excited cries and guffaws of onlookers outdone by the furious roar of a teamster as he heaved on the reins to prevent his heavy wagon running down the deputy who now had an arm caught in the horse's reins and was being dragged into the street.

A man stepped in front of Lane, looking beyond him towards the clamour, and was thrust aside. Another man, quick on the uptake, grabbed for his shoulder and took a punch on the chin. Gasping, Lane jumped off the plankwalk and went across the street, caused a rider to veer sharply — and a shot rang out. A bullet hissed by, then a second. The deputy had freed himself, and was in pursuit, but because of the people between them he was forced to aim high.

A horse, Lane thought. I need a horse.

Think, man, think. When they brought the buckboard in with the wounded Ben they'd left their horses at the corral owned by John Behan. Nate had likely collected his and ridden home. Could be he had taken Lane's, not expecting it to be needed. On the other hand . . .

A swift glance behind told him the deputy was not gaining. And he was still unable to get a clear shot. The corral was, what, a hundred yards away? But there could be no mistake about where he was heading, and in the time it took him to find his horse, throw on a rig, the deputy would be on him.

But what else could he do?

He could steal a mount, he thought, as he ran flicking a glance at the hitch rails, the dozing horses — ready saddled, maybe with a Winchester in the boot. He had slowed, had his eyes on a lean sorrel outside a gunsmith's, was turning towards it when common sense screamed a warning. If he tried that, the people in the streets who were unwittingly shielding him from the deputy would turn against him: they would see a horse-thief, pounce, and he would be finished.

Then, suddenly, he was at the corral.

The old hostler was outside his office. Lane rushed past, gasping, 'My horse!', saw the man's mouth fall open and his vague gesture down the runway and ran into the cool shadows. Where? Which goddamn stall! He stopped running, stood panting, chest heaving, turned one way then the other, felt the cold sweat trickle down his back and his mouth suddenly dry — and knew it was no use.

He was too late, had no time.

At the far end of the runway, two figures had stepped in out of the sunlight. Quent and Seth Colquhoun. Metal glinted in their fists. Behind him, a shadow fell long down the runway as the deputy came in from the street. Even as Lane turned towards him, he heard the oily click as the Colquhouns cocked their pistols. He lifted a hand to the deputy, felt the skin on the back of his neck prickle, took one more step — and a mighty blow slammed into the back of his skull and it was as if his reaching arm stretched into an infinity that was forever beyond his grasp as his senses faded and he was swallowed by bottomless blackness.

Part Two

The Traitor

9

Ching . . . Ching . . .

Lane Condry, the Last Chance Kid, reached up with a shaking hand to dash sweat from his brow. The sun had poked its rim high above the eastern hills, the cactus and dust scent of the desert was already strong in his nostrils at the clear promise of the coming heat. The clink of hooves on stone as the riders drew near was an annoying distraction that made him shake his head as he ducked down, slid into a sitting position with his back against a rock and tried to gather thoughts that were in turmoil.

The morning's warming air breathed its balmy touch on his sweat-damp skin, but inside he was as cold as the grave and the sound that was driving all others into the background — hooves on stone, the indistinguishable, menacing murmur of hard voices, the oily snap of a rifle hammer cocking — was the tinkle of those damned Mexican spurs at every movement of the tall rider's horse.

When had he first heard them? Eight weeks ago, his pa with a slug in his shoulder and sweating under the doctor's knife after the dawn raid in the San Pedros, Nate alongside him as Quent Colquhoun had said amiably, 'You watch your tongue, boy', and walked away from John Behan's corral and livery barn in Tombstone with spurs jingling.

He'd heard those spurs again when Colquhoun walked away from the hush that followed the violence in the Oriental Saloon, cards scattered across the table, Jack Kenyon in his chair bloodied and dead; heard them yet again at noon the next day when Quent Colquhoun walked in to pay his brother's fine and walked out into the Tombstone sunlight as Lane listened to Justice of the Peace Wallace sentence him to twenty-five years in the pen.

After that had come his own break for freedom, the violent blow delivered by an unknown assailant — not a bullet from the Colquhouns, or he wouldn't have made it this far — his later transport to the penitentiary and endless days followed by sleepless nights when the darkness pressed down on skin glistening with sweat and his eyes stared blindly into a future without hope.

And then, yesterday, he'd again heard the music of the spurs.

'Wait there,' Nate had said softly. 'Keep your head down, don't move away no matter what. I'll be there before dawn with a good horse, food, a six-gun. I cain't do no more, but I figure it's enough to see you across the border. It's a chance, maybe the last you'll ever get, kid . . . '

In Yuma State Penitentiary. Visiting. A sweating, thickset guard standing close with a shotgun, but not close enough to hear those soft-spoken words or the ones that had preceded them.

'A guard's been bribed. Sometime between now and midnight he'll make himself known. When he does, go with him, trust him.'

And then as Nate walked away from him, his first visitor in the eight weeks since Justice of the Peace Wallace had passed sentence and now destined to be his last, Lane had posed the question.

'Where the hell did you get those spurs?'

Nate had turned, grinning, and winked at the guard. 'Let's say Quent Colquhoun objected to something that happened in Behan's Livery barn, and I ended up with a couple of souvenirs.'

'You were there?'

'You know where I was. I was in the hollow up in the San Pedros, in the barn with Pa, Ma hiding up in the loft, all of us waiting for that dawn raid that never happened — but it couldn't, could it, seein' as you'd conveniently killed the man threatening our family.'

Shocked despite himself at that cold

voicing of a falsehood, Lane had let it slide, already aware that protestations of innocence were a dime a dozen in Yuma.

Instead, he said, 'The Colquhouns were acting for Jack Kenyon, Quent shot Pa and now you're wearing his spurs. What gives you that right? How close were you and those owlhoots, Nate?'

But Nate Condry had simply tugged thoughtfully at his dragoon moustache, shaken his head and turned away with a faint, enigmatic smile.

'Just remember what I told you,' he said as he went out and the barred door clanged shut; and Lane had watched him go, listened to the music of the spurs . . .

And wondered.

★   ★   ★

The wondering was over.

A trap had been set; dressed in another man's clothes he had run straight into it and sat shivering as night turned to day and the trap's jaws snapped shut. The man who had arranged his freedom and sent him running like a scared rabbit to the arroyo in the Yuma desert was his home-loving elder brother, Nate Condry, a pillar of righteousness who had lost $5000 playing poker with a man who had died in suspicious circumstances; and the extent of his brother's treachery not only planted a numbing sickness in Lane's soul but raised a whole series of questions.

For eight weeks Lane had been convinced that Quent Colquhoun was the man who'd snatched his pistol in the darkness of the Oriental and framed him for the shooting of Jack Kenyon. He had never understood why, and was no nearer to reaching the answer — but now he had another name to play with, a more tangled plot to unravel.

Jack Kenyon had made a dawn raid into the San Pedros, and given the

Condrys an ultimatum. On the subsequent trip into town with the wounded Ben Condry, Lane had witnessed a brief exchange of words between Nate and Quent Colquhoun; between the two of them there had been a comfortable familiarity. Perhaps because his own life had been lived among men whose nature it was to lie and scheme, that easy camaraderie between his brother and a maverick had aroused his suspicions. He had asked a question in the Oriental Saloon, and an indirect answer from Ace Jardine had told him that Nate was a poker player — which suggested Quent Colquhoun was just one of a number of renegades and owlhoots with whom Nate must have rubbed shoulders.

Hours later, when a man stood accused of cheating and blackness descended as Abe Colquhoun smashed the oil lamp over the card table, a chair had scraped, and gone over with a bang. About that there was no mistake. Then Seth scraped a match, another flared as Ned Boyle lit the lamp at the bar — and all the chairs, occupied and unoccupied, were in place. Not counting the murdered Jack Kenyon, the men seated were Ace Jardine and Nate Condry. And Nate had sat and watched in silence as Lane stood accused, had —

Snapping through Lane's thoughts, driving him up on to his hands and knees in the dust to peer down through the rock cleft, three spaced shots cracked out in the still desert air.

Some way below, a rider was clattering out of the arroyo. A quarter mile away, near a cluster of tall saguaros, others were holding their horses on tight reins but letting them wheel as the slapping echoes of the shots died away and Nate Condry holstered his six-gun.

As the men came together and conferred, voices drifted to the Last Chance Kid.

'He's around somewhere, on foot, and hungry,' Nate said, his voice rising and falling, thinned by distance. 'If he got the location wrong, he'll hear those shots and come looking for me.'

'If we spread out we'll spot him quicker when he comes out of his hole, get this over and done with,' a second man said, and Lane's eyes narrowed as he recognized Abe Colquhoun and, alongside him, backing up his words with a nod of the head, his son, Seth. The other three men were strangers, unshaven hardcases on ragged ponies, Yuma men recruited for this killing who hung back with hard, watchful eyes.

Nate thought for a while, lifted his eyes so that Lane could have sworn he was looking directly at the rock cleft, then nodded. 'We'll do that. Col, you stay here, keep your eyes open. The rest of us'll ride straight out for maybe a mile, like the spokes of a wagon wheel, come back in on a zig-zag course that covers a lot of ground.'

The man who had ridden out of the arroyo stepped down from his horse. The other five riders swung their mounts and set off at a canter across the desert, the riders radiating from the hub that was the arroyo where Lane Condry should have been found, pulling five plumes of dust that hung and settled behind each man like the morning mist that had been dissipated by the heat of the fast rising sun.

In that vast landscape they swiftly became tiny and indistinct, swallowed by their awesome surroundings, masked by dust and the beginnings of the shimmering heat-haze.

The man called Col watched them go, poured water from his canteen into his Stetson, gave his horse a drink then let it wander on trailing reins towards a patch of parched vegetation in a shallow, cactus-fringed hollow. A fine horse, Lane noted, deep chested, with legs built for speed and a spring in its step that suggested it was still fresh despite the run from Yuma. Col watched it walk away, then slapped moisture from his hat, planted it on his head and sat down in the shade of one of the saguaros — and that was the last Lane Condry saw for he was already off his knees and snaking his way down from the high ground.

As he moved away from the cleft that for several hours had been his cold, lonely eyrie, he was driven by the knowledge that a couple of hundred feet below there was a man with a horse and a gun who had searched the arroyo that had been the arranged rendezvous and pronounced it empty. That man was confident enough — foolish enough — to close his eyes and doze in the sun, but the other five riders were alert and would fast be approaching the mile distance laid down by Nate where they would swing their mounts and head back.

And with racing pulse and a shiver of apprehension, Lane Condry sensed that this was not only a race against time and a mighty hazardous chance of escape from the tight net cast by Nate — it was his first chance, and his last chance!

He went leaping and tumbling down from the heights with the rocky spine of the slope between him and the man with the Stetson tipped over his eyes as he dozed under the saguaro. His speed was tempered by the need for silence. Loose stones were avoided with nimble footwork. He sought out the pockets of dust between knife-edges of rock and planted his feet firmly in them to deaden his footfalls. And all the time as weight and momentum threatened to tip him over and his arms flailed for balance he was blanking out the harsh rasp of his own breathing and the hissing hammer of his pulse to listen and monitor the progress of the distant riders — too close, surely too close — and detect any movement from the man who, through his inability to see beyond the most obvious hiding place, had gone from hunter to hunted.

The slope of the rocky hill brought Lane out into the open some fifty yards to the right of the oblivious man. He stopped there, bent forward with hands on quivering thighs, calming his breathing, dashing sweat from his brow. Again and again he cursed the lack of a weapon — then cursed himself for wasting time and breath. A weapon was within reach. He had the cunning, and the guile — but did he have the time?

There was no way of knowing.

His hectic tumble from the heights had deprived him of his eagle's eye view of the desert. The haze of dust left by the riders still hung in the now hot air, and without the flattening effect of a high viewpoint the seemingly level landscape had become a mass of undulations beyond which Nate and the four riders could be a mile away, or racing back to dash his only chance of breaking out of the trap.

Move, move!

And he moved, impulsively, and fifty yards away the horse grazing on coarse grass lifted its head and looked straight at him.

Lane froze.

The horse whickered softly, and

lowered its head.

The man, stretched out, hat over his face, stirred and crossed his legs — and settled to stillness.

There was the soft shudder of expelled breath as Lane again straightened from his crouch, watched the hunted man through eyes slitted against the sunlight, then sprang into action.

Between them there was the merest suggestion of a rise. Lane went for that at a dead run. He ran with legs and arms pumping, his eyes fixed on the reclining figure with the beckoning gleam of a six-gun at his hip. His course was arrow straight. The rise was never likely to be enough to shield him if the man caught the sound of his approach but, psychologically, it was reassuring. So he ran at it, over it, and down the slight slope, dust spurting from beneath his racing feet, the disturbance caused by his fleet passage no more than the merest whisper of sound.

The horse was standing watching him with white-rimmed eyes, muscles quivering, ears pricked.

And then the man moved, lazily flipping his hat back and rolling easily sideways to come up on an elbow.

To face the other direction.

He had caught the sound of approaching hooves.

In the same instant, Lane heard the faint drumming. It was as if the beat of hooves came from all around him, still distant, but there nonetheless like a noose drawing tight. And as he heard that sound and felt freedom slipping away from him he stretched his legs and covered the last remaining few yards, sucked in a breath, opened his mouth and let loose with a screaming, Rebel yell.

And launched himself in a full length dive to hit the startled man with a bone-crunching thud.

The man grunted. The impact drove him flat. He took a mighty, looping right fist to the jaw, a left that peeled back the skin from an eyebrow, another right that followed through with a spray of bright blood. But this was a man who had brawled in bars from New Mexico to the Gulf, held his own against pistol and knife. On his back in the dust he spat out a broken yellow tooth and grinned at Lane, brought up a bony knee that slammed into Lane's thigh, reached out a clawed hand to rake Lane's eyes.

It was as if an angry cougar had caught him with a flailing paw. He jerked back his head as strips of fire scored his cheek, fell backwards in the dust with hot blood salty on his snarling lips and lashed out with both feet. He heard the crack of leather on bone, saw the man's leg crumple even as he struggled to rise. As he went down, a hand stabbed for the six-gun. Pivoting on one hand, Lane spun in the dirt. Again he launched a savage kick. This one caught the man on the side of the head. His eyes glazed. The hand making the draw lost its way.

And Lane pounced. He could hear a feral snarling and knew it issued from his own throat. He clenched his teeth on the ugly sound, drove a desperate punch at the man's throat. The man gargled, gagged. His hands came up, clutching at his windpipe. There was a thin, keening whistle as he struggled to suck in air. As his eyes bulged, Lane made a dive for the holster, plucked the six-gun free and slammed the barrel across the side of the struggling man's head. The skin split. He went down soundlessly and lay still, breath hissing wetly.

On his knees, the Last Chance Kid unbuckled the man's gunbelt and slipped it off, wrapped it around his own waist as he came to his feet and ran for the ground-tethered horse.

As he did so the whisper of approaching hooves became a rattling tattoo on the hard desert earth, rose to a swelling thunder in his head, and suddenly the fine, strong horse that stood with flared nostrils watching his stumbling approach looked as far away and unreachable as the distant San Pedro Hills.

10

The horse's sleek muscles quivered under the soothing hand, its hooves shifting nervously on the stony ground as it prepared for flight, its eyes rolling wide as the other hand came up to grasp its muzzle. Its sides were heaving. It would have tossed its head and jerked free if Lane Condry's gentling hand had not ceased its ministrations and moved to hold the cheek band firmly, close to the metal bit; held tight while he whispered soft words of reassurance that were little more than meaningless sounds but were nevertheless understood.

The horse became still. Man and beast stood locked together. Each, for his own different reasons, was rigid with apprehension and fear.

The race from the tall saguaros to the arroyo had been short but swift, a breathless sprint across 400 yards of hot, open ground as Lane drove the horse at a dead run and the menacing thunder of the approaching hooves swelled within his skull and crawled under his skin to send his pulse crazy. Once there, once in the deepest section of the shallow ravine, the only section where he could be certain a full-grown horse would be well below the level of the surrounding desert, he had dismounted. And now, he knew, his survival was in the lap of the gods.

Nate and his men had ridden away in different directions, and were returning over the same ground. The man who had traced the arroyo's rim with his horse's dancing hooves as he rode into the desert would do the same on his return. If he looked ahead to the place near the tall saguaros where the man called Col had been left — where that man now lay unconscious, or dying — then all would be well and Lane would have bought precious minutes of time.

He had gone some way towards buying the time he would need to get clear of his hunter by dragging the unconscious man deep into the cluster of saguaros, dumping him in the shade and kicking dust and stones over him so that he became as one with the landscape; became a rock among many rocks.

But if the man now drawing near looked down into the dry wash . . .

Preceded by the rattle of hooves, the rider came in fast, even closer to the arroyo, if that were possible. In one instant there was nothing above Lane Condry but the flat expanse of hot blue sky. In the next, horse and rider exploded into view, dark shapes blotting out the sky as the rider pushed the horse hard along the jagged edge and Lane was looking up at flashing hooves and the wet flanks of a lathered roan, listening to the horse's ragged breathing and eating its dust — then ducking back as loose stones flew like bullets.

For an instant he thought he was as

good as dead as a hoof slipped on the loose edge, the racing horse snorted its fear and the man snarled an angry warning and wrenched hard on the reins to pull his mount's head around.

And then, as fast as they had appeared, they were gone.

Danger had passed Lane by in four or five short seconds.

The way was clear.

For a few more seconds he stood listening. The sound of hooves had faded into silence. Voices could be heard. All the riders had returned. Then, heart hammering, Lane took the horse at a walk along the length of the dry wash. It was a snaking fifty yards long, and because of the land's contours Lane knew that for most of the way they could not be seen by the men now gathered at the saguaros.

Fleetingly, it occurred to him as he walked and sweated that by hiding the man called Col he had given reason for those men to lift their heads and resume their search, this time for their companion, and increased the risk of his being spotted.

Then he pushed those fears into the background. He had taken the man's horse. They would assume he had ridden away. The last place they would expect to find him would be in the dry wash he had already searched. They would be looking elsewhere.

And then the wash petered out ahead of him and he was leading the horse up the end slope and . . .

Softly, stealthily, Lane trailed the reins before the horse emerged from the wash, moved away from it and sank to the ground to look back towards the saguaros.

The heat shimmered. Dust hung in the air. Close to 500 yards away, ground tethered horses stood with dropping heads, tall cacti were wavering shapes standing with arms outstretched. Beneath and around them, men were moving. As Lane watched, he saw them come together to move into the saguaros, and knew that he had hidden the man but not the tracks in the dirt that pointed the way.

He saw them find what they were seeking; drop down to examine the stricken man —

Now!

He sprang to his feet, ran to the horse and leaped into the saddle. As he scooped up the reins and wheeled away from the arroyo he heard distant shouts, knew without looking that they were sounds of anger and confusion, not triumphant discovery of their quarry. He also knew that would come, and swiftly, desperate to put space between him and his cold-hearted brother, he cruelly raked the flanks of his valiant horse with his heels and drove it out into the heat of the open desert.

He drove it towards the east. He drove it hard and fast, and horse and rider maintained that pace during a long sustained spell when Lane Condry looked back more than he looked ahead. But as the day dragged on, and behind him the desert remained as empty of life as the searing vastness that lay ahead, Lane felt his shoulders relax, felt panic recede, felt the growth within him of a stubborn resolve and the recognition of the enormity of the task that lay ahead. That task was not simply a matter of staying ahead of relentless pursuers, nor was it the successful traversing of 300 miles of desert and mountains that lay between him and the San Pedro Hills. The task that lay ahead of Lane Condry was of convincing Ben and Nan Condry — if they were still alive — that their eldest son had betrayed his family, then of finding out the reasons that lay behind that treachery and bringing Nate to justice. If he could not succeed, Lane could not clear his own name and would forever be a man on the run from the law.

For the Last Chance Kid, the day of final reckoning had arrived.

11

The fist was like a steel hammer, the hard knuckles smashing into his jaw with the full weight of the powerful shoulder behind them, knocking him back against the wall. His head sang. He felt the trickle of blood in the three-day stubble at the corner of his mouth, lifted a finger to test his teeth, found the familiar, coppery taste and managed a smile.

'Pa, you know damn well that won't change anything.'

'Makes me feel better. Maybe makes you understand you don't walk in here and call my son a liar, no sir, you don't do that, you *won't* do that.'

'More than a liar. A man prepared to have his own brother killed and Lord knows what else, but — '

'No, Ben!'

Nan Condry's face was white. She

stepped forward swiftly, placing herself between Lane and her enraged husband who had cocked his fists and pulled back the right for another wild swing.

'But we have to talk about it,' Lane finished, and gently took hold of his mother's shoulders and moved her aside. 'If we do that, maybe we'll understand what he's done, why he's done it — and if we don't reach that understanding here, tonight, then tomorrow we start searching until somewhere, somehow, we come up with some answers.'

'I won't waste time arguing with you — '

'Talking. Like grown men.'

'My God!' Ben's fists clenched and unclenched as he stood stiffly in front of Lane. He swung away, violence in his every movement, and went to his seat by the stove. As he sat down his hand reached out for his pipe, but he was so blind with rage that he knocked it off the cold stove and the stem snapped as it hit the hard dirt floor.

'Grown men,' Ben echoed scathingly, and he tugged his Stetson tight over his eyes. 'That, from a man who spends so much time away he's a stranger in his own home, turns up out of the blue to murder a man in cold blood and see treachery in his own kin.'

'I did not shoot Jack Kenyon. And three days ago Nate bribed a guard to get me out of Yuma, then came after me into the desert with a bunch of armed men. Why would he do that?'

'You're mistaken.'

'Ben, he's just walked through the door and he's worn out. He needs food inside him, time to draw breath — '

'There *is* no time, Ma.' Lane moved away from the wall, sat down wearily in the chair usually occupied by Nate, noted his father's fierce look and went on doggedly. 'I'm an escaped convict. Word will have reached Tombstone. We need answers now, before the law gets here.'

'Or Nate.' There was contempt in Ben's voice. 'If Nate went into the desert after you, he'll come after you here. The fact that he ain't done that yet proves my point.'

'Nothing's likely to be proved unless you two get together,' Nan said. 'I'll get Lane something to eat. And Ben, you sort this mess out — and do it like a gentleman, not one of those . . . those damn ruffians that are behind all Nate's troubles.'

As she left the room Lane saw a flicker of amusement in his father's eyes at the mild curse that, for Nan Condry, was so out of character, and for a moment they were silent in a shared intimacy. But for Lane that pleasurable warmth was short-lived; the importance of what his ma had said lay in that final word, and he pounced on it.

'Troubles?'

Ben stretched up to a shelf, felt around, found another blackened pipe. 'Nothing to speak of.'

'Pa, come on, help me with this.'

'He got to gambling, went out nights. You were away, so you wouldn't know.'

Ben was looking down, concentrating on tamping tobacco in the pipe's bowl. 'Nothing serious, but me and your ma were against it. I guess we figured a boy brought up to work horses would be no match for gamblers and rustlers and cold-blooded killers.' He shrugged, struck a match, held the flame over the bowl.

'You were right,' Lane said softly. 'He lost ten thousand dollars in six months.'

Ben's eyebrows shot up. 'No. That can't be.'

'It came out when John Behan was questioning me after the Kenyon shooting. When Nate played poker, Ace Jardine was usually at the table. By his reckoning, that's how much Nate owed Jack Kenyon.'

'Kenyon!'

Ben was holding the match poised and, as he repeated the dead businessman's name in shocked tones, Lane saw his eyes go distant and imagined the riot of suspicions that must suddenly be racing through his brain. He waited, dabbed at his bloody lip with his bandanna, saw the match burn down to his pa's fingers and heard him curse softly and drop the blackened stick.

'According to John Behan,' Lane said, 'Nate had ten thousand good reasons for wanting Kenyon dead.'

'When we talked in those bad days before they took you to Yuma, you were of the opinion Quent Colquhoun used your pistol to shoot Kenyon. Are you now saying it was Nate?'

'I don't know. Thinking back to that night in the Oriental, I remember Colquhoun next to me, on his feet, then the light going out. In the darkness, I heard someone yell, and a chair go over. In those few seconds — ten, no more — someone used my six-gun to shoot Jack Kenyon. But when Ned Boyle lit the lamp, everything was as it had been. Quent Colquhoun was standing, all the chairs were in place, Nate and Jardine in their seats.' Lane paused, listened to the faint rattle of dishes in the kitchen, shook his head. 'I'm sure it was

Colquhoun — but he could have been paid.'

Smoke curled from the bowl of Ben Condry's pipe. His anger had gone as swiftly as it had flared.

'All right, let's say he was. So who had reason to want Kenyon dead?'

'If thieves stick together then just me — for what he was doing to my family — and Nate, to wipe out gambling debts.'

Ben shook his head. 'You're forgetting Lee Kenyon. He inherited his pa's business. Nate's gambling debts still stand.'

'Has Lee Kenyon been pushing him?'

'Not that I know of.'

'Then there must be other reasons.'

'For what?'

Lane drew a breath. He had left Nate, Abe and Seth Colquhoun far behind when he rode away from the arroyo, had pushed on for most of three days, always watching his back. But every mile of the way on the southerly route along the Mexican border to

Nogales and north to Tombstone he had been looking for answers, for the motives that lay behind a young man's treachery, and if in that time he had come up with none — in almost seventy-two hours had reached no conclusions — then how could he answer his pa?

'One more question,' he said. 'Quent Colquhoun plugged you in the shoulder, and Kenyon vowed to be back next morning to run us all out of the hills. When Nate showed up at Yuma Pen, I asked him if he had been here to help meet that threat. He said yes, he was with the two of you, in the barn.'

Ben's eyes were stricken. 'Your ma was with me in the house. Nobody came. We didn't see Nate until two days after Kenyon's death.'

'Then I *think* Nate was behind the killing of Jack Kenyon,' Lane said. 'When I turned to face the deputy at Behan's Livery barn, somebody gun-whipped me from behind — and your answer tells me that was probably Nate.

I know Nate got me out of Yuma, then tried to kill me — but you're asking me why, and I can't give you an answer.'

'Then quit wasting time and go talk to Lee Kenyon.'

This was Nan Condry. She had emerged silently from the kitchen and now, having said her piece, she placed a steaming plate of fried steak and eggs on the table and stood with hands on hips. Her face was flushed from the heat of cooking. She held herself stiffly upright as she looked at the two men.

'Why?'

'Ben,' she said, 'I've been listening to every word spoken in this room, but the only thing we know for sure Nate's done wrong is lose a heck of a lot of money playing poker. The man he owes that money to is Lee Kenyon. Start there. But, one way or another, find out if your sons — yes, both of them — are honourable men, or no good liars and cheats.'

'I'll start there,' Ben said, 'if you insist. But leaving you alone goes against the grain. If Jack Kenyon lusted after this land, his son will be doing the same — and things have been quiet for so long I'm getting uneasy.'

'There's not a lot they can do to empty property. If they come here when you're away, I'll hear them a mile off and walk into the hills.'

'I'd be a fool to believe that,' Ben said. 'What you'll do if they come is stand at the window with that Sharps and drop anything that moves.'

'That's Ma's choice,' Lane said with a thin smile. 'Like I said at the beginning, we talk, and if we don't come up with the answers then tomorrow we start looking. That's the way it's turned out — and Ma, God bless her, has pointed the way.'

★   ★   ★

The three Kenyon silver mines were in the bald country to the north, east and west of Tombstone, but the company's offices were in a dilapidated building on

Allen Street, between a general merchant and the Nevada Boot and Shoe Store. Lee Kenyon was a man who saw no link between profit and hard work, and even when his father was alive he had kept a room at the Cosmopolitan Hotel, worked out of the Tombstone office but spent most of his time in either the Oriental or the Eagle Brewery.

That night, while Lane was polishing off his second plate of steak and eggs, Ben Condry had pointed out the problems posed for them by Lee Kenyon's lifestyle. The new owner would be somewhere in town, not out at the mines; the telegraph wires would be humming with the news of Lane Condry's break, so it would be foolhardy for Lane to be seen on the streets of Tombstone; yet they had to see Kenyon.

Again, Nan Condry stepped in with a suggestion: the two men should leave the San Pedros well before dawn, and be in the Kenyon Mining Company's office waiting for young Lee when he arrived.

'Break in the back way, when the town's asleep,' Ben Condry had said, and he had winked at Lane and looked at his wife with new-found respect for her cool head and clear thinking.

Thus it was that Lane Condry found himself on Fremont Street when the cocks were beginning to crow, cutting through the vacant lot between Fly's studio and the OK Corral and leading his pa along the back of the buildings fronting Allen Street.

'Hard to tell from here,' Ben said, easing his horse to a slow walk as he scrutinized the anonymous timber walls.

'This one.'

'How so?'

'Those grain sacks tell me the general store's next, and this one stinks of leather.'

Ben grunted his agreement, swung his horse in and stepped out of the saddle. Lane followed and, as they tied up to a rotting timber post, he eyed the building. The wan light of dawn revealed a back yard littered with trash, windows thick with cobwebs, an unpainted door with a single rusting padlock — clearly never used.

His pa had already bent to dig the rusty head of a miner's pick out of the trash. As Lane reached him he took a mighty swing and smashed the padlock. Metal clanged as Ben dropped the pick. He pulled the door open, its rusty hinges creaking. Lane slipped past him and stepped into darkness.

And listened.

In the gloom he could see sagging cardboard boxes, rolled maps, an oil-lamp hanging from a beam. The room was small. The door in the opposite wall led to the front office — he guessed.

A wagon rolled past along Allen Street, but in that packed storeroom no sound disturbed the thick silence.

Behind him, Ben pushed impatiently. A pile of cardboard boxes rocked as

Lane passed. One fell with a heavy thud. Thick dust tickled his nostrils. He sniffed, touched the latch of the inner door, eased down with his thumb. Carefully, he pushed the door open — and stepped through.

'If you hadn't spent so long away,' Lee Kenyon said, 'you'd know on poker nights I sleep in the office.' On the far side of the room away from the two desks and the bookcases he was sitting up on a leather chaise, chest bare and glistening in the faint light seeping through the windows overlooking Allen Street, a blanket up to his thick waist, his black hair tousled.

The shotgun he was holding was cocked, and steady. It was pointing straight at Lane Condry.

12

'If you're going to pull that trigger,' Lane said, 'at least tell me what the hell's been going on between my brother and the Kenyon family.' He let a thread of anger and desperation leak into his voice, deliberately held the man's gaze with his own. Yet as he spoke — and from the edges of his gaze watched nervously as Kenyon's big knuckles gleamed bone-white on the big scattergun's triggers — he was listening for stealthy sounds in the storeroom behind him, praying that his pa was also listening hard and thinking his way out of trouble.

And, faintly, he caught the whisper of cloth brushing against the hard cardboard of stacked boxes; felt a faint draught on his neck as a door opened; heard the muffled click of a latch.

'Let's call it ambition aided by a

pressing need,' Lee Kenyon was saying, snapping Lane back to the immediate danger. 'My ambition, Nate Condry's pressing need to get rid of weighty debts.'

He came up off the chaise, a big man light on his feet, swept the blanket away with one hand to reveal crumpled dark trousers. The shotgun's twin black muzzles wavered not an inch. He looked at Lane, still standing in the doorway leading to the back room, grinned, and placed the shotgun on the desk.

'Hair trigger,' he said matter-of-factly. 'It's pointing your way; all I need to do to blow a hole in your belly is jar it with my fist.' And, still retaining the ghost of a smile, he hit the desk gently with the side of his hand to add weight to the warning then picked up a pure white shirt, slipped into it, fastened the buttons and tucked it into his pants.

'I suppose,' Lane said, playing for time as he watched a shadow drift lazily past the front windows, 'having your pa killed wiped out Nate's debts and left the way clear for you to take over the mines?'

'No.' Kenyon shook his head, rammed his feet into tooled leather boots and went around behind the desk. 'Your brother's debts still stand, and he's got a heap to do yet before they're worked off.' He had been busy opening drawers, slamming them shut. Now he held up a sheaf of papers, dropped them on the desk and Lane saw scrawled IOUs, figures with a lot of zeros, his brother's name.

'You're a ruthless bastard, Kenyon.'

'Ain't that right!' He grinned. 'And now I've just caught me the man who was convicted of murdering my pa, and escaped from Yuma.'

'I was wrongly convicted.'

'The longer the trail and the more men die, the less chance you have of coming up with proof of innocence.'

'So it *was* Colquhoun used my pistol?'

Kenyon ignored the question, sat

down in a swivel chair, idly reached out with a forefinger to move the shotgun butt so that the muzzle swung in a back and forth swathe on the desk.

'The killing was arranged by you,' Lane persisted, 'with me the man going down for a crime he didn't commit. For the sake of money, you and Nate are both walking roughshod over our families. But why implicate me?'

'You're wasting breath,' Lee Kenyon said, 'when you're pretty close to drawing your last.'

His hand slipped up the shotgun's stock, reached the trigger guard — and froze there as footsteps clattered on the plankwalk, became muffled as the approaching men leaped down into the dirt of the street. The running feet came to a standstill. Something hard began pounding on the door.

'Do it now, if you've got the guts,' Lane said, meeting Lee Kenyon's eyes, 'because, by God, you'll never get another chance.'

'Kenyon, open the goddamn door!'

'John Behan,' Lane said. 'I guess the time you had's all run out.'

'I'm legally justified,' Lee Kenyon said through his teeth. His black eyes were glittering, flicking towards the door, then back to Lane Condry. 'The way it stands you're an escaped convict, I'm within my rights to blow — '

A boot slammed into the door. The lock splintered. The door was driven back hard to hang shuddering against the wall. Lane saw none of it. His eyes were fixed on the shotgun with its hair triggers, the muzzles lined up on his belly, the big man's fist holding the deadly gun close to the trigger guard. Then, as the beefy, goatee'd figure of Sheriff John Behan burst in from the street closely followed by Ben Condry, Lee Kenyon's fingers relaxed and he sat back away from desk and shotgun.

'Take him away, he's all yours,' he said to Behan.

'It ain't quite that simple,' Ben Condry said breathlessly, and he winked at Lane. 'It seems Justice of the

Peace Wallace exceeded his authority. He had no legal right to convict my boy, send him to Yuma without a fair trial.'

'Didn't he, by God!' Kenyon leaned forward, made a move for the shotgun.

'Leave it!'

Behan's voice cracked like a pistol shot. Kenyon's hand stopped, poised over the Greener.

'He killed my father,' he said. 'Are you telling me he goes free?'

Behan eased the door shut, holstered his pistol and sank into a chair.

'What I'm saying is the whole damn town and its judicial system got so tied up over the OK Corral killings it lost its way. If it hadn't been for that, Condry would have been out of Yuma weeks ago, and up before Judge Wells Spicer and a sworn jury.'

Moving away from the storeroom door, Lane said, 'I was framed for Kenyon's killing, Behan, and I think the men responsible expected me to be locked in the Tombstone jail awaiting

153

trial. That's the way they wanted it: they had plans to kill me before I reached a court. Wallace ruined everything by sending me to Yuma, so in eight weeks they came up with another bright idea, sprang me from the pen and tried to gun me down in the desert.'

'Bribed a guard, I hear.'

'He walked me straight out the door.'

'Your brother behind it?'

'He worked the Yuma trick, with Abe and Seth Colquhoun along to do the killing — but Kenyon here's already admitted he's got Nate in a stranglehold because of gambling debts.'

'Which is not an excuse for a man to turn against his own kin.'

'No, but it means my brother's a small fish in a big, muddy pool.'

'Well,' John Behan said, 'you can't say you didn't ask for it. You picked Ace Jardine's brains, went after Kenyon, got mixed up in a card game and dragged into something a sight too deep for you.'

'And ended up killing my pa,' Lee

Kenyon said. 'Anything else said here is just wasted talk.'

He'd left the desk and was over at a cabinet pouring whiskey into a cut crystal glass. He tossed back the expensive liquor, pulled a face, glared a challenge at Behan.

'*Somebody* killed Jack Kenyon,' John Behan corrected, 'when Abe Colquhoun doused the lights in the Oriental and two men were close to Lane Condry. One was Quent Colquhoun. If Quent did the job, he did it with his pa's help. Now I'm told Abe was out at Yuma with Nate Condry. So the picture I'm getting is of two men working a killing — one now dead — and a man roped in by gambling debts. But who's behind it?'

'We know who holds those promissory notes,' Ben Condry said softly, looking meaningly at the desk. 'Is the same man calling the tune, paying the wages?'

'I don't have to listen to this,' Kenyon said. 'I'd like you all out of my office.'

He slammed the glass down, went to the open front door and stepped outside, stood stiffly looking along Allen Street.

'The man you've got to worry about,' Behan said to Lane, 'is Marshal James Grey — but he won't roll out of bed for another couple of hours.'

'What about you?'

Behan shook his head. 'I've stated my opinion. You were wrongly convicted, and you've got the right to come before a jury. Maybe the verdict'll be the same, but I guess you'll take that chance.'

Ben Condry had wandered across to help himself to Kenyon's whiskey. He paused, glass raised, and said, 'What exactly are you suggesting, Behan?'

Behan stroked his pointed beard, his eyes thoughtful. 'You rode in nice and early. If I haven't seen you I'm damn sure nobody else has — and I'd say Lee Kenyon's got his fingers in too many pies to go rushing to James Grey.'

'Haven't seen me?'

Behan grinned at Lane. 'You're not

here, Condry, not you or your pa.'

Ben left the drinks cabinet, nudged his son, and together they went through the storeroom and out the back door. The waste ground was still deserted, their horses where they had left them. They mounted up, swung away and clattered back across that stretch of open ground to Fremont Street and headed out of town. They met a wagon coming in, the teamster giving them not even a glance. And it was only after they had put a couple of miles between themselves and Tombstone that Lane Condry called a halt, pulled into a patch of scrub that stretched its shadows long before the swiftly rising sun, and realized he had no idea where to go, or what to do next.

★   ★   ★

Ten minutes after they had stopped, smoked a cigarette and mostly spent time alone gazing into the distance and

157

mulling over a muddle of disturbing thoughts, Ben raised the alarm.

'Five riders, comin' hell-for-leather from town.'

'So Kenyon didn't go to the law,' Lane said, flicking away his cigarette, 'he went straight to his cronies.'

'That include Nate?'

'Maybe. All I know for sure is me being locked away in Yuma wasn't enough — he wants me dead, and I don't know why.'

'I've got some ideas on that,' Ben said.

'Like?'

'Like, putting the blame square on Lee Kenyon. That feller ain't too fussed about going against an old horse trader and his wife, but throw the Last Chance Kid into the equation and he can see problems.'

'I was locked away.'

'And Nate got you out, probably had no choice. But if he could do that, who's to say you couldn't have done it on your own. Kenyon wasn't prepared to take that risk, have you come after him.'

'Seems to me you've come around to accepting Nate's involvement in this, but attribute no blame.' Lane flashed his father a rueful grin, received a noncommittal shrug in return, then ducked instinctively as something buzzed wickedly overhead and was swiftly followed by the crack of a rifle.

'Mount up,' Ben snapped.

'And go where?'

'Head for home.'

Lane shook his head. 'That'll lead them to Ma.'

As they swung into the saddle, Ben cast a black look in Lane's direction. 'Supposin' some others are already there? Maybe she made it into the woods, maybe not — but I intend to find out.'

Lane felt a sudden twinge of fear. He swung his horse away from the patch of scrub and spurred after his father. A thin yell rang out, but the voice was faint for the riders were still some way behind. A second bullet whined. Then there was a rattle of rifle fire and Lane and Ben Condry flattened themselves along their horses' necks and concentrated on putting distance between themselves and their pursuers.

They cut towards the north and west, and after two miles of flat out riding Lane realized that, despite his words, his pa was heading diagonally away from the San Pedro Hills. He cast a swift glance behind him, saw the faint pall of dust now much further behind and said a silent prayer of thanks for Ben Condry's excellent stock of horses.

'Ease off,' he called.

He caught up as Ben slackened his pace. Riding stirrup with his pa, he said, 'If you want to pull them away from the San Pedros, that doesn't need two of us.'

Ben flashed him a look. 'If we split up and I head for home, they're just as likely to follow me.'

'Not if I drop back and cause trouble.'

'Too risky — and it might not work.'

Lane squinted ahead, casting his eyes back and forth over the bleak terrain.

'They're too far back to see clearly. There's an arroyo over to the east. That's the wrong direction entirely, and should fool them. When I drop back and kick up some dust, you ride over that way and keep out of sight; when I start shooting, they'll think we're still together. Once their heads are down, I'll ride due north, pull them away from you. When the way's clear . . . '

Ben twisted in the saddle, squinted back towards the distant riders spread out across the arid plain, and nodded.

'What you were saying before, about blame: Kenyon was right, there's a mining family's ambition, a desperate man sucked into the mess and betraying his family because he owes money.'

'I think there may be more. We don't know what threats Jack Kenyon and his son used to twist Nate's arm, turn him against his family.'

'If this works out,' Ben said, 'maybe we'll find out.'

He reached across, touched Lane's shoulder, then swung his horse and walked it away to the east. Lane wheeled his horse and headed back the way they had come, riding hard, veering his mount from side to side like an agile cutting horse to kick up a dust cloud. After a couple of hundred yards he drew rein and stepped down. He took the rifle from its scabbard, checked the loads, then hunkered down alongside a tall cactus.

He fired three fast shots at the approaching riders, saw a man's hat go flying and other men pile out of the saddle and hit the dirt, ran thirty yards to the right and fired another three; back again, fired twice more then ran for his horse and leaped into the saddle.

The ground sped beneath flashing hooves as he drove the eager horse from standstill to a flat out gallop and tore away towards the north. Again he made his direction erratic, lifting a wide swathe of drifting dust that was more likely to have been kicked up by two riders than one. And he didn't look back. He rode hard and fast, flattened in the saddle, gambling on being followed and wanting to put as much distance between himself and the arroyo where his pa was lying low.

In the end, he knew it had been a mistake. When, after another two hard miles, he did slow down and look over his shoulder, the land behind him was bare of any living creature — and there could be but one answer: the men who had followed them from Tombstone had ignored the shots, and the fleeing rider, and had turned towards the San Pedros. And Lane was left with the stark and painful realization that by opting not to head straight for home, he and his pa had allowed Lee Kenyon and whoever was with him to get ahead of them.

Like brother Nate, Lane Condry had gambled, and lost.

13

It took an hour's hard riding for Lane to catch his pa, riding across country to cut him off, his hat-brim flattened by the wind and salt sweat in his eyes as he looked ahead to the thin, hanging dust cloud that could have marked the passing of friend or foe. The sun was high and glaring, burning the back of his neck. The ground over which he rode was featureless, but deadly: jack-rabbit holes lay in wait for a stray hoof, and would snap a horse's leg; rocks laid bare by the erosion of sun and wind could turn a horse's ankle and send the rider toppling in a breakneck fall.

He caught him as Ben was pushing his horse up the first slopes of the San Pedros, drove his own lathered mount alongside and was met by a savage glance from eyes squinting out of a lined face masked by dust.

'Figured wrong,' Ben said, teeth flashing. 'The bastards ignored you and me both. I hope to hell your ma took off into the woods.'

'If she didn't, she'll hold them from the house.'

'I counted four riders. She's got a single shot Sharps. They'll eat her alive.'

They pushed on, not talking, ears straining so hard they ached. On the snaking trail half a mile below the notch in the hills, they heard the boom of the Sharps, the crackle of six-gun fire, and Ben cursed softly. But his horse was wrung-out, could go no faster — was close to failing. Forced to ease back, they worked their exhausted horses up the steep trail listening to a spatter of gunfire from the unseen hollow, then to a silence that was almost too painful to bear.

The shot, when it came, took Ben's horse from under him, dropping it on its nose and flinging Ben wide and sprawling in the dust. Instantly swinging off the trail and into the trees,

Lane saw the puff of smoke in the high pines on the notch's east shelf, the quick flash of sunlight on metal. A glance told him that Ben was clear and safe, scrambling away from the dead horse clutching his Winchester. Then a second shot kicked up dust, and Lane swung out of the saddle and dragged out his rifle.

Ben came panting into the trees, blood trickling from a grazed cheek-bone.

'You see him?'

'No — but hoist that Winchester and keep looking.'

Lane levered a shell into his rifle, took aim, fired. The shot drew an instant response. Bullets snicked through the low branches. The muzzle flashes were clearly visible, the dark shape of a man either confident or just plain foolish.

With a grunt, Ben triggered three fast, aimed shots. They both heard a strangled cry. Then a rifle came clattering down from the shelf and now, over its edge, an arm hung limp and lifeless.

'All right, we'll go in the hard way,' Ben said.

Lane left his horse and followed his pa up through the trees, marvelling at the older man's stamina, struggling to keep pace as Ben clawed and clambered his way up the uneven slope that took them over the ridge to the east of the notch. Gasping for breath, sweating, fighting their way through tough grass and matted undergrowth, they passed the dead man — a stranger — sprawled on his back under the pines staring glassy-eyed at the clear blue skies, breasted the high rise and started on the steep down slope that formed one side of the bowl where Ben Condry had made his home.

'Easy,' he said, peering ahead as he held out a restraining arm.

On this side of the ridge there were few trees. What there were, they used for cover. Then they petered out. They stayed back in that thin fringe. Ahead of them lay a naked slope of some fifty feet, the open yard — the house.

'We downed one. I see Abe and Seth Colquhoun,' Lane said softly.

'And Kenyon.'

Lane nodded. Both Colquhouns were mounted, backed off across the yard holding the reins of a riderless horse. Lee Kenyon was on foot, close to the house, shotgun held loose in his hands as he talked. The window through which, on the night of his return from the Eagle Brewery, Lane had seen the warm glow of lamplight — Lord, was that just a couple of days ago? — was shattered. A rifle barrel poked over the sill. It was trained on Kenyon's chest.

'Stand-off,' Ben said, and there was pride in his voice. 'Nan won't listen; Kenyon can't go forward or back.'

'A bad thing to say,' Lane said, 'but if Kenyon wanted this thing done right he should have brought Nate.'

'Maybe he did,' Ben said. 'At first sight, didn't I say five riders?'

'So if the fifth man was Nate — where is he?'

'He's the one man who knows this place so well he could sneak in the back way.'

'You think he'd do that to his own ma, come up behind her . . . ?'

Lane let the words trail away, numbed by their import, and Ben shrugged, his eyes bleak.

'We'll worry about that later. Right now we need to let Kenyon know he's in trouble.'

'We could pick two of them off,' Lane said, 'before they know we're here — and I don't think Kenyon could stomach that.'

Ben grunted, and shook his head. 'That's not my way, never has been.'

Kenyon had stopped talking. He turned away from the window, and began to walk away. The rifle poking over the sill stayed steady, but no flame spurted from the muzzle, no bullet slammed into the mine-owner's back.

'Not Ma's way either,' Lane said.

'Sometimes I wonder how you two survive.'

'We get by right well,' Ben said. 'And what you and me are doin' now is something drummed into me by my army superiors: we're holding the high ground.' He grinned at Lane, indicated that he should stay back in the trees, and turned to look across the yard.

'Lee Kenyon!'

Ben's unexpected bellow cut through the hot, dusty air, and from the hollow three pairs of eyes snapped towards the hillside, raked the slope. Kenyon was caught like a man with his pants down, halfway between house and horse. But Lane's assessment of the man's character was wrong. Far from being fazed by his predicament, Kenyon swung to face the slope, lifted the Greener and let go with both barrels of the big scattergun. His aim was good. Lane and Ben fell flat as shot whined like angry hornets and hot lead peppered the trees. As they hit the ground and slid on their bellies on grass and pine needles, Abe

Colquhoun let go of the loose horse's reins, spurred across the yard while dragging out his six-gun and blasting wildly. Seth was doing the same. Suddenly, Lane and Ben were grovelling in the dirt on the edge of the trees, looking at two riders tearing towards the slope some way apart and with Kenyon standing firm in the centre cramming fresh shells into the Greener.

Flat on his face, spitting out pine needles, Lane reached for his six-gun — and found an empty holster. He swore, twisted to look back into the trees. Metal gleamed in the dappled sunlight. As gunfire crackled he wriggled around, heard a thump and a soft grunt alongside him and flicked a glance towards Ben. He was down and limp, face white, mouth slack with pain. As Lane turned again and his outstretched hand clawed desperately for his pistol, a wild slug caught it and sparks flew as it leaped out of his reach.

Then the two riders hit the slope.

They drove their horses up the hill

with wild Rebel yells, six-guns spitting flame. Lane came up on his knees, twisted, then dived towards his pa. He was fumbling for the downed man's pistol when Abe Colquhoun thundered across the slope towards him, leaning out of the saddle with his six-gun extended to bring him so close he couldn't miss.

Then his horse went down.

Lane was lying awkwardly on his side, struggling to cock his pa's six-gun. Colquhoun was coming fast, ten feet away, his grinning face like a death mask. Then his horse's knees buckled and Abe was flying through the air. The horse hit the ground, stirrups flapping, blood pumping from a gaping wound in its neck. There was the sudden stink of dust and blood, the acrid bite of gunpowder, the sound of bubbling breathing as the horse died; the echoing crack of a distant rifle that came again as a second bullet slammed into the ground inches from the dazed Colquhoun's head.

Then Lane was on him. He covered ground at a crouching run, swung the pistol, slammed the barrel across Colquhoun's cheek and lost his balance as he saw the sudden bloody gash as the skin split. He could hear the panting snorts of the second rider's horse as he closed in, heard as if from afar the regular crack of the distant rifle, heard Kenyon scream out from the yard. Then Colquhoun rolled and lashed out with a booted foot that slammed into Lane's fork and sent a bolt of agony shooting up through his belly.

Curled in a ball he rolled, breath hissing through clenched teeth. He slammed an arm out to stop himself, again grunted in agony as Abe Colquhoun, on his feet and running downhill, stamped on his hand. Lane's roll brought him into a sitting position, facing downslope, arms wrapped around his knees. Clamping his teeth against the urge to vomit he saw, through streaming eyes, Abe hit the yard in a staggering run as Lee Kenyon spurred towards the notch. Seth Colquhoun had already spun his mount and sent it bounding back down the slope. At the yard, he pulled the horse back on its haunches long enough to hook his arm into Abe's and heave him up behind the cantle. Then he spurred after Kenyon.

And suddenly, there was silence.

A faint haze of dust and gunsmoke hung over the yard. As if of its own volition, a stone rolled down the slope, and came to rest. In the trees, a branch creaked in the hot sun, and the beat of receding hooves was the faintest of whispers lingering in the hot, still air of the San Pedro Hills.

★ ★ ★

'A scratch,' Ben said. 'An old man crying over nothing.'

This was soon after Lane had helped him down the slope and into the house, and with the sun streaming in through the window he and his ma had stripped off Ben's red-soaked shirt to examine the wound and at once ruled out the long trip to Tombstone. All that pounding in a buckboard, Nan said, would do more harm than good, and she'd brought boiling water and clean white cloths and dressed the long, bloody groove the bullet had raked across Ben's back from shoulder to shoulder.

Half an hour later he was tightly strapped and sitting in his chair by the cold stove puffing at his gnarled pipe. Despite the heat of the day all three were clutching mugs of hot, sweet coffee, and the one subject left unbroached was the one uppermost in their minds.

Lane was of the opinion that they had witnessed Lee Kenyon's last gasp. The son, he pointed out, had ruthlessly used Quent Colquhoun to remove Jack Kenyon with the aim of grabbing everything for himself, but had turned out to be his father's weak shadow. To take by force what was not legally his he needed the backing of cold-blooded shootists, ruffians like the Colquhouns; to succeed as a mining man, he needed business acumen and a cool head, but had neither.

'My guess,' Lane said, 'is one of the bigger mining companies will make an offer, and Kenyon will grab it with both hands.'

'Which just puts the fist of iron in another man's glove,' said Ben.

'No. We'll take one day at a time, just like you've been taking life all these years since you moved up here from the river. But remember, in all that time the only trouble has come from Kenyon, and there's no reason why men who've left us alone up to now should suddenly change.'

'Kenyon would have wiped us out,' Ben said thoughtfully, 'but for that unknown gun.'

'It was Nate.'

From his brother's chair near the window, Lane looked at his ma. 'We don't know that.'

'I do. I told you before you rode out this morning the only thing we know for sure he's done wrong is lose money over the poker table. Well, you spoke to Lee Kenyon and all that did was stick a burr in the seat of his pants and send him plumb loco — if he wasn't already there. You've told me nothing new, so I'm forced to believe what my senses have witnessed: I heard that rifle, I saw its effect — and the man pulling the trigger saved our lives. Who else do you know would want to do that?'

'That,' Ben said affectionately, 'is just about the longest speech you've ever made, and I must admit it carries some weight.'

'I'd like to believe it, too,' Lane said, 'but behind me I've got the vision of Nate astride his horse in the Arizona desert, those damn spurs of Quent Colquhoun's jingling as he sent his gunmen out hunting me.'

'I'm not disputing what happened,' Nan said, 'but I'll always believe there's an explanation we're just too blind to see.'

Lane shrugged, put down the coffee mug and came out of the chair to stand restlessly at the window. 'If that rifleman *was* Nate and he was out in those trees hoping to pop Lee Kenyon, I could understand it . . . '

'The first slug took Abe Colquhoun's horse,' Ben said, 'and that was about as far away from Kenyon as it could get.'

'It was Nate,' Nan said stubbornly, 'and he was out there saving your lives.'

Ben took the pipe out of his mouth and looked at his son's back. 'If you're right, we've got little to fear from Kenyon. He's made his bid, and failed. If word gets around — '

'It will,' Lane said, swinging to face the room. 'I'll ride into town this evening.'

'Why leave it that late? At that time, lawmen will be gettin' busy, other powerful men finished their business and out of town.'

'Two reasons,' Lane said. 'First is, I

want to watch you for the next few hours. Fever could set in. You take a turn for the worse, you're going to need the doc.'

Nan planted her coffee mug on the table, stood up and moved to her husband's side. 'And second?'

'If it was Nate out there, I'd say he's pretty mixed up. I'd like to give him time to make up his mind. Make his choice. Them or us.'

'Dammit, Lane,' Nan said fiercely, her hand on Ben's shoulder, 'that boy's just proved whose side he's on, what else do you need?'

'Helping us by shooting from cover takes courage, but I reckon walking through that door after all that's happened takes a lot more.'

'He's up to it,' Ben said.

'Then I'll give him until dusk. If he's not here by then a whole lot of things could be wrong, and the only way I'll find answers — good or bad — is by riding into Tombstone.'

14

Dusk fell over the hollow, and in the way of the desert country was swiftly followed by an inky darkness that dropped like a heavy curtain from clear skies sprinkled with a million glittering stars. A chill came with it and, as the cooling timbers of the Condry house creaked a comforting accompaniment to the snores of the deeply sleeping Ben Condry, Lane kissed his ma, for an instant rested the back of his hand reassuringly against her hot cheek then went out to saddle his horse.

No Nate. But had he honestly expected him to come walking into the house? Did he honestly believe that the man who had pulled the trigger of the rifle that had knocked Abe Colquhoun's horse out from under him as he came up the slope had been his brother?

As he rode away from the warm lamplight and out of the hollow to slip through the notch and swing his horse towards distant Tombstone, Lane knew that if the answer to the first question was a resounding no, the answer to the second was an equally resounding yes — yet for the life of him he could find no explanation for Nate's actions.

The most logical was that he had seen the error of his ways, was trying to make amends but was too ashamed of what he had done to show his face. But, from the outset, Nate's actions had not been directed by logic, and the most sensible comment yet made had come from the wounded Ben Condry: 'If that rifleman out in the trees was Nate,' Ben had said, 'and he was out there hoping to pop Lee Kenyon — I could understand it.'

Well, Lane couldn't argue with that. Turning up his collar and deftly rolling a cigarette as he rode, he fired it up, blew a trail of smoke over his shoulder and tried to apply logic to actions that seemed to defy reasoning yet, on closer examination, bore the ring of inevitability.

When Abe Colquhoun and his brother had ridden across the hollow to charge up the slope, shooting Lee Kenyon would not have saved Lane and Ben. Nate — if it was Nate out there — had an instant to decide, and had gone for Colquhoun's horse.

Clearly, he could have ridden into the yard at any time after that, walked into the house and been welcomed by Nan with open arms. But — still applying logic — the torment of overwhelming debt that had driven Nate from the family home and seen him set up his own brother's murder still hung over his head. Although Ben's spur-of-the-moment comment seemed to condone Nate's popping Lee Kenyon, deeper thought would convince him that was no solution. In the saloons of Tombstone, Nate's debts were public knowledge. If Lee Kenyon was gunned down, Sheriff John Behan would go after Nate.

An hour down the trail, his thinking still as clear as a muddy pool, Lane pulled off, dismounted and let his horse graze. He rolled another cigarette, lit it, then almost at once took it from his lips. The taste in his mouth was sour, acrid, and he knew it came not from tobacco, but from confusion, apprehension, and not a little fear.

Could be they were chasing rainbows. He laughed softly. Yeah, if he used logic, that's what it would come up with: stop kidding yourself, Lane Condry. A few shots from an unseen rifle had convinced Nan her boy was pure as the driven snow, led Ben to believe he was — rightly or wrongly — hunting down Lee Kenyon, and sent Lane looking for explanations down a road paved with logic that had more cracks in it than the hard-packed mud of Fremont Street and the OK Corral.

But all that was pure fiction.

Nate had gone bad. He'd had a hand in Jack Kenyon's murder, had sprung

Lane from Yuma because killing him would ensure the vein of silver beneath the hollow would be guarded by just Ben and Nan, and as long as those debts hung over his head he'd dance to Lee Kenyon's tune.

That was truth. That was logic. But neither of those two abstracts could tell him where Nate was, or what he would do next, and with a soft, bitter curse, Lane Condry flicked away the acrid cigarette, remounted and rode towards Tombstone and an uncertain future.

★ ★ ★

From a mile out, the treeless plateau across which Tombstone sprawled was sprinkled with lights that in the stillness of the night were like warm reflections of the stars in unseen pools. But there had been no rain. From half a mile the lights became smoky lanterns, the noise from the saloons — scores of them — a cacophony that tore apart the natural stillness and peace of that scene and set a man's nerves jangling.

If he was a cowboy or a mine worker looking for excitement, the listener would thrive on that tingle of anticipation and put his horse to a gallop. But for Lane Condry the raucous clamour dried his mouth and set his pulse uncomfortably thudding as, half a mile out, he passed the shallow depression where lay the sprawled buildings of a Kenyon silver mine and pushed on up the naked slope towards the first shabby buildings.

Fremont street was ill lit. He looked ahead to the Papago Cash Store and Bauer's Union Market, contemplated riding that far to cut across the OK Corral. But uncomfortable vibrations beset his mind with dark shadows — it was too soon after the bloody gunfight, too many ghosts still afield — and instead he turned into Fifth Street where high false fronts cut off any of the sky's luminosity. The blackness was lit by yellow lamplight spilling from the Oriental Saloon and the Eagle Brewery

— and the tension was electric.

Why?

It was midnight. Up ahead, a figure started across the road. Lane eased his horse back to a slow walk. For an instant he thought it was Nate, and opened his mouth to cry out. Then he clamped it shut. It was a drunk, weaving from side to side, a tall man but unprepossessing, and Lane turned away to look along the hitch rails for Nate's horse.

Voices again snapped his head around. The man, full to the gills with hard liquor, had been stopped by a dark-suited man who had turned in from Allen Street. This time he was someone Lane recognized: Lee Kenyon. And the glint of metal at his side suggested he was still toting the big Greener, or a long gun of some kind.

Lane eased himself out of the saddle, stood so that he was hidden by his horse's bulk. The two men were talking in low voices, the words muffled, indistinguishable. But it was clear that

186

the other man, despite his intake of whiskey, was disagreeing violently with what Kenyon was saying.

Then the man turned, angrily shaking his head. Lamplight caught his face, and Lane saw that it was Abe Colquhoun. That the two men were out at midnight at once screamed a warning at Lane. As they continued to argue he again turned his gaze anxiously towards the hitch rails and saw Nate's horse, hipshot and dozing amongst the others outside the Eagle Brewery.

So what was Kenyon asking of Colquhoun? And where was Seth? As the two men seemed to come to an impasse and both began walking towards Allen Street, Lane led his horse across the street, loose-tied it and tried to put himself inside Abe Colquhoun's mind.

The man was a rustler, frequently violent, and on that night in the Eagle Brewery he had sat at the same table as Jack Kenyon and raised the possibility of driving the Condrys off their land by force. But since then, much had happened. Only hours before that dawn raid was to be launched, Abe Colquhoun had drawn back his hand and thrown the whiskey bottle that had plunged the Oriental Saloon into darkness. When the lamps were lit, Jack Kenyon was dead — and whoever his killer might be, the balance of power had shifted. Suddenly, the silver mines were owned by Lee Kenyon. It seemed certain that Abe Colquhoun had played an active part in his murder — but had he miscalculated? Had he killed the golden goose believing that in the offspring he had a chance of doubling his stake, only to discover that Lee Kenyon was shallow, useless at business, unpredictable — and dangerous?

Thoughtfully, Lane patted his horse, stepped under the wooden awning and pushed through the swing doors to blink in the sudden glare of gleaming oil-lamps and the bite of cigarette smoke that hung like foul swamp mist over the tables and bar.

Comparatively quiet, even for the hour after midnight. A couple of men were standing drinking at the end of the bar, laughing softly from time to time as they chatted to a painted sporting girl. At a central table a high-stakes card game was in progress, but lazily, the faint snap of cards louder than the jingle of silver dollars and the murmur of the bids. Ned Boyle was behind the bar, polishing glasses, watching the doors.

More memories. A man called for his cheating. Breathless stillness as footsteps sounded overhead. Sudden darkness and the crack of a shot, Abe Colquhoun at the bar, the lamp over the table smashed and dripping coal oil. Ned Boyle's match flaring, the spread of wet blood over the front of Jack Kenyon's white shirt.

Now, at that same table, with a bottle of whiskey and a glass, Nate Condry sat watching his brother.

Lane let his breath go with a shudder. He went to the bar, got a second glass from Boyle, sat down at the table. He poured whiskey, raised his glass to Nate, drained it; poured a second and stared at the pale liquor as fire warmed his belly.

Nate broke the uncomfortable silence.

'Did I hear shooting?'

'Your ears are playing tricks.'

'To be expected. There's been more than enough gunfire the past couple of months.'

'Or maybe you're looking darkly into the future.'

'Maybe I am.'

'Then snap out of it.'

Nate laughed. 'If he's lived in Tombstone the past few months, most nights a man'll go to sleep haunted by dead men, the names of Clantons and McLowrys echoing in his head. No recipe for optimism.'

'Nor is the passing of time in Yuma State Pen, which is where I've been lying sleepless and without hope.'

'Right. And if it wasn't for me, you

wouldn't be here now.'

'Goddamn it!' Lane said. 'Wasn't it your actions put me there in the first place?'

'You think I stepped alongside you to take your pistol, pulled the trigger, shoot Jack Kenyon?'

'Did you?'

'No.' Nate reached for the bottle, poured a drink. 'I warned you, don't you remember?'

'Yeah. 'Lane, you watch your back', you said. All that tells me now is you knew what was about to happen, were in it up to your neck.'

'And now I'm out.'

A chair scraped as one of the poker players left the table and went to the bar. A ragged cough drew Lane's eyes, and he realized it was Seth Colquhoun, his dark eyes briefly passing over the two brothers. The rustler leaned against the bar to speak to Ned Boyle. Boyle's eyes flicked towards the table where Lane sat with Nate. He shrugged, passed a fresh pack of cards to

Colquhoun, followed him with his eyes as he returned to the poker game, then went back to his patient door watching.

Why, Lane wondered. What the hell's going on?

To Nate, he said, 'Isn't it a bit late to bow out?'

But Nate's mind was elsewhere. 'If you're wondering,' he said, 'they — we — are expecting Lee Kenyon.'

'Ah.' Lane nodded slowly. 'If he's after your blood, then it must have been you out there in the hills.'

'And as for being late bowing out of this mess,' Nate said, 'that would depend on when the decision was made.'

'I'd guess this afternoon, round about the time you rode out to the San Pedros with Kenyon and saw for yourself what he was about to do — which is pretty late.'

'How about when Quent Colquhoun pulled the trigger and plugged Jack Kenyon? Pretty late, I'll grant you, but sometimes it takes an incident like that to clear a man's head.'

'But if you're telling the truth, none of what's happened after that night makes any sense.'

Nate grinned. 'You never were much of a thinker.'

Lane dragged out his tobacco, offered it to Nate, saw the shake of the head and began rolling a cigarette.

'Let me try,' he said, fingers busy. 'Lee Kenyon wanted his pa out of the way and used Quent Colquhoun, assisted by Abe. It wasn't planned for that night, but me stepping into that poker game and calling Kenyon a cheat made it easy. Then, instead of heading for home, you hung around. You saw me marched in front of that fool Wallace, watched me and the deputy play hide and go seek, and stepped in to knock me to the ground when it looked like — '

'Yes, I did that. For your own good. You know Quent and Seth would have gunned you down, deputy or no deputy. Hell, you were on the run, they were justified. Seemed to me unconscious was better than dead, the state pen better than choking at the end of a rope.'

Lane put the cigarette on the table and sipped his whiskey, eyes narrowed thoughtfully. All right. Quent and Seth were there, what Nate had done could be put down to quick thinking. But that only explained why his escape had failed, and the way Nate was talking . . .

'Let's get this straight. Are you telling me I was deliberately taken in front of Wallace, and he was paid to pass the lighter sentence?'

Nate nodded. 'By Lee Kenyon.'

'On whose say-so? It wasn't his idea. Kenyon would want me hanged. So who?'

No answer. The question hung in the smoky air. Nate's eyes were amused.

Feeling his way, Lane said, 'That first night I was in the Eagle watching Jack Kenyon's table and listening to them discuss driving Ben out of the hills, a mutual friend was mentioned.'

This time, Nate's laugh was ironic. 'Is that what they called me? I owed a heap of money; I was someone they could use.'

'To drive your own family from their home?'

'It didn't come to that, still hasn't. You know damn well I was there both times those Kenyons tried, and took no part in it — or, if I did, it was on the side of justice and fair play. That first dawn, when the shooting started, I warned Kenyon to back off. Damn it, I saw you watching me!'

'I saw your signal, sure. But why would Kenyon back off at your say-so?'

'Jack wasn't Lee, was nothing like him. He wanted Pa's place, but without bloodshed. I was suggesting with that one shot he'd done enough, the rest would be easy.' Nate lifted his glass, drained it, grimaced with distaste and pushed it across the table. He looked at Lane, spread his hands. 'Today . . . well, Lee Kenyon was never going to back off, and you saw what happened when

Abe Colquhoun rode up the slope.'

Lane sighed. 'All right. You're making your own treachery sound like a goddamn crusade, but apart from standing by while your pa takes a slug in the shoulder, and almost leaving it too late today — yes, I guess it's fair to say you did nothing to be ashamed of. And if you did somehow get Kenyon to bribe Wallace . . . ' He left the words unfinished, picked up the cigarette, rolled it in his fingers then struck a match, applied it and sucked in the bitter smoke. 'But that,' he said, trickling smoke, 'brings us to something that cannot be explained.'

'Think about it,' Nate said.

'I have, time and again.'

'You think you could have ridden away from that arroyo at Yuma if I hadn't planned it that way from the start?'

'This is what I think: if you planned to set me free, you would have come to Yuma alone — '

'The guard was *Colquhoun's* buddy.

To get Abe to agree to a bribe I was forced to bring him along with Seth and those Yuma toughs, point you towards the desert and set you up.'

'Then why did they hang back when I roughed up their pal — what was his name, Col? — and rode away?'

'For the same reason Lee Kenyon wanted you dead. Your reputation. Hell, you must have been watching, listening, from wherever you were hiding. I played along with them but split them up, deliberately left Col back at the arroyo on his own. When we got back you'd downed him like I knew you would, and now you were out there with his horse and weapons. I asked Colquhoun what the hell Kenyon had ever done for him that made risking his life against the Last Chance Kid a reasonable proposition.'

The cigarette smouldered in Lane's fingers. He stared at the glowing tip, knew that everything Nate had said made sense, knew that there was no way he could have ridden away from

the Colquhouns if they'd been determined to follow him into the desert and
run him down. And it was as if an
immense weight had been lifted from
his shoulders. The whiskey he had
drunk on an empty belly was hitting
him hard, he could feel its warm glow
and the relaxation of mind and body
that it induced was making his eyelids
heavy and, as Seth Colquhoun made a
bid and the poker players murmured
and the cards lazily snapped and money
jingled, Nate crossed his outstretched
legs under the table and Quent
Colquhoun's spurs went ching, ching.

But this time the sound was comforting, not sinister. Lane lifted his eyes,
met his brother's level gaze, saw the
light smile playing under the dark
dragoon moustache and said, echoing
Nate's words, 'Quent objected to
something you did in Behan's Livery
barn. I guess that was slugging me on
the head. You wearing his spurs means
he got ugly, made his play — '

'And was too slow.'

'And Seth figured he was next and ran for it.' Lane nodded. 'So why did you get me out of Yuma?'

'Because I'd been sick of outlaws and rustlers and ruthless businessmen since that night in the Oriental, been done with the lot of them. Because a gambling debt had begun to look pretty small weighed against my family's future. Because, although he would never admit it, our pa, old, proud Ben Condry, needed the Last Chance Kid. And still does.'

'Now? Why now? You said you were expecting Kenyon here. You think maybe he'll make another try? At night?'

'I don't see him,' Nate said.

'Then,' Lane Condry said tersely, 'I think you and me had better head home — and fast!'

15

Gunsmoke lingers, and in a town like Tombstone it is a trustworthy harbinger of all things evil.

They went out through the swing doors on to Fifth Street and, over and above the cooling scent of the desert, the gunfire that Nate had heard — for there is always gunfire in Tombstone — was recalled by the hanging stink of its cordite. That pungent reek at once sent a message to the brain that pumped adrenaline into the bloodstream and set the pulse racing. Lane felt the hairs on the back of his neck prickle. The urge to run was almost irresistible, but there was nowhere to go. Lamplight from the Oriental and the Eagle pooled the street, but faintly, and beyond that wan lake of yellow light the shadows were deep and impenetrable and filled with unseen menace.

The horses at the rail blew softly, shifted restlessly sideways. Eyes rolled white. Ears were pricked.

'Your horse is across the street?'

'Right.'

Lane watched Nate stride away towards the Eagle Brewery, flicked a glance sideways towards Fremont, the other way towards Allen Street. Nothing moved. He stepped towards his horse, touched its warm neck and flicked the reins free of the rail, backed it from between two nervous horses and swung it around.

He had the reins bunched and his hand on the horn and was fumbling, looking down into the shadows as the toe of his boot chased a swinging stirrup, when the shot cracked.

Nate was almost across the street. As the startled horse jerked, pulled the reins taut and sent him staggering, Lane saw his brother stop like a steer that has hit the end of a dallied rope. He jerked upright, went down backwards, rolled, and lay still.

Caught cold, for an instant Lane froze. Instinct told him to run to his downed brother; caution and common sense held him back. Then, as the reek of fresh gunsmoke drifted to his nostrils, he felt a boiling surge of anger that tightened his jaw and set his pulse hammering in his ears, sent his clawed hand towards the butt of his six-gun.

'Kenyon!'

Lane let his anger loose in a violent surge as he roared the killer's name, then slapped the horse's rump, drove it back towards the hitch rail and moved recklessly into the centre of the street until he was close to where Nate lay dead.

'Kenyon, show your face!'

The flash had come from an alley some sixty yards away, close to Fremont Street. Now, at Lane's shout, a bulky dark figure stepped out of the shadows. A gleaming rifle was in the crook of an arm. A pistol jutted from a thigh holster.

'Now throw away your rifle. There's

only one way to settle this.'

'Me against you?' Kenyon barked a laugh. 'Make it sound attractive, Condry.'

'All right. Ditch the rifle. Then walk towards me. You're free to start shooting, anytime. You won't get answering fire from me until you're within twenty yards.'

'Be kinda foolish to say I don't trust you.'

'And there's only one way to find out.'

Kenyon's teeth flashed in the lamplight. He stretched out his arm, and the rifle fell with a clatter. He reached down, drew his six-gun and pulled back the hammer — and all the time he was watching Lane.

Lane Condry, the Last Chance Kid, made no movement.

Lee Kenyon lifted his cocked six-gun, and pulled the trigger.

The flash was a brief, dazzling flare. The bullet was a whisper of sound far to Lane's left.

'That the best you can do?'

And now Kenyon was walking. He was a big man and, like all big men, he moved with lightness and grace. The sixty yards became fifty. He stopped. Cocked the pistol. Fired.

A bee droned, not too close, and in an instant had flown away.

'Four slugs left. And you've got thirty yards.'

'Poor odds, Condry.'

'Like my brother, I'm a gambler.'

'In case you missed it, he just lost.'

Kenyon was talking, and walking. Without warning, he fired. The bullet winged wide.

'He's dead,' Lane said, 'and now you'll pay — '

Again the pistol flashed. Something plucked at Lane's sleeve. He felt the dryness in his mouth, a twitch in his fingers — and forced himself into stillness as Kenyon advanced another ten yards.

'That's twenty yards,' Lane said through stiff lips. 'You've got a couple of slugs left, but you've run out of room. One more step — '

'Your brother's alive,' Kenyon said.

'Pull the other one.'

'Take a look.'

'Sure, that's what you want.'

The mine-owner's son was so close that, in the bright light that suddenly washed from the Oriental, Lane could see the sheen of sweat on his heavy face. Nervously, the big man's eyes flicked left, then back to Lane. His six-gun was level. Now, it swung sideways, pointed down towards the dirt of the street. The hammer went back with an oily click.

'I'm right. Your brother moved again. Now, stretched out like that, real close, he'd be hard to miss — wouldn't you say?'

On those last three words Kenyon's voice was raised almost to a shout, and Lane felt the power of the man, the weight of his terror. Was this, he wondered, what they called a stand-off? His six-gun was in its holster. Kenyon's was cocked, and aimed. Lane Condry was the Last Chance Kid, and had faced a dozen similar situations in a dozen shabby streets. But in every one, the cocked gun he was facing had pointed at his own belly, the risk he faced when he stabbed a hand for the slick butt of his pistol was that if he was too slow, he died.

Could he gamble with Nate's life?

The seconds dragged by. Lee Kenyon was grinning, but it was a twisted, frozen grin, and on the trigger of his six-gun his finger was bone white.

If I don't make a move, Lane thought, he'll snap. He'll snatch at the trigger, and Nate will die.

Across the intervening twenty yards he looked into Lee Kenyon's eyes. In their glossy sheen, there was a pinprick of light, the reflection of lamplight spilling from the Oriental. As Lane stared, that pinprick of light went out.

Now!

As Lane's hand stabbed for his pistol, Kenyon's eyes again flicked left. To

Lane Condry, his draw was extended interminably. It was as if the signal from his brain took an age to reach the muscles of his hand and arm, those muscles were deathly slow to respond, and when they did they moved with the speed of a man living a dream in slow motion.

Yet, in the end, nothing mattered.

Halfway through that draw that seemed to last for all of eternity — so in the space of what could have been no more than the merest fraction of a fraction of a second — a shotgun thundered. Lee Kenyon, who would in any case have been left for dead by the speed of Lane's draw that in reality was like greased lightning, was dead. He was driven backwards with his face a shocked mask, his chest a torn and bloody mess. And as he hit the ground and the pistol bounced high from his lifeless, outstretched arm to fall spinning and fire with an impotent crack on impact with the hard dirt, Lane reeled sideways from the double-barrelled blast and looked towards the Oriental.

The pinprick of light in Kenyon's eyes had died when a man stepped out of the saloon and cut off the lamplight. Seth Colquhoun. He was standing in the doorway. In one lean hand, a shotgun smoked. In the other, a hand of poker was still fanned. Across that distance he looked for a long moment at Lane Condry. Then, as if nothing had occurred, he swung about and went back inside to the pot he would almost certainly win.

'It's over. Kenyon's dead. Our home's safe.'

That was Nate, croaking, but alive.

Lane dropped to his knees. There was blood on the downed man's shoulder, but the eyes were bright, colour was flooding back into lean cheeks, and under the dragoon moustache there was the trace of a brave smile.

'I can understand Kenyon,' Lane said, 'but why would Seth do that?'

'Can you think of an easier way for him and Abe to get a silver mine?'

Lane took a breath. 'I told Pa another mining company would make an offer. But I guess that offer Seth just made couldn't be refused . . . '

He leaned down, grasped Nate's good hand and pulled him to his feet and, with the scary feeling that what he had lived through had been a reckless man's last chance — and with the certainty that it was the last time he would put it to the test — Lane Condry once again took an injured man across Tombstone to be treated by the long-suffering Doc Gillingham.

And already the light of a new day was visible in the east and sending its washes of pale colour over the distant San Pedro Hills.

THE END

We

re

Did y

ar

We publish a wide range of high
quality large print books including:
**Romances, Mysteries, Classics
General Fiction
Non Fiction and Westerns**

Special interest titles available in
large print are:
**The Little Oxford Dictionary
Music Book, Song Book
Hymn Book, Service Book**

Also available from us courtesy of
Oxford University Press:
**Young Readers' Dictionary
(large print edition)
Young Readers' Thesaurus
(large print edition)**

For further information or a free
brochure, please contact us at:
**Ulverscroft Large Print Books Ltd.,
The Green, Bradgate Road, Anstey,
Leicester, LE7 7FU, England.
Tel:** (00 44) **0116 236 4325
Fax:** (00 44) **0116 234 0205**